Something Understood and Other Stories

Something Understood and Other Stories

Short stories by
Dr Ajaya K Upadhyaya

BLACK EAGLE BOOKS
Dublin, USA | Bhubaneswar, India

Black Eagle Books
USA address:
7464 Wisdom Lane
Dublin, OH 43016

India address:
E/312, Trident Galaxy, Kalinga Nagar,
Bhubaneswar-751003, Odisha, India

E-mail: info@blackeaglebooks.org
Website: www.blackeaglebooks.org

First International Edition Published by
Black Eagle Books, 2024

SOMETHING UNDERSTOOD AND OTHER STORIES
by **Dr Ajaya K Upadhyaya**

Cover & Interior Design: Ezy's Publication

ISBN- 978-1-64560-594-2 (Paperback)
Library of Congress Control Number: 2024948273

Printed in the United States of America

*In memory of my father - a man of few words, but on
whom the value of sensible speech was never lost*

All art is at once substance and symbol.
Preface to **The Portrait of Dorian Gray**
Oscar Wilde

Preface

Stories are a vital part of the human condition, and storytelling has a rich history. Although I have enjoyed reading stories all my life, the urge to write came to me relatively late. The unprecedented pandemic in recent years caused unspeakable misery for many and wrought havoc in the lives of most of us. But, as the proverbial silver lining to the cloud, the reclusiveness it imposed resulted in an atmosphere most conducive to creativity.

The pandemic provided an opportunity for my foray into creative writing and several stories in this collection were written during the lockdown. Cut off from our customary contacts and routine social diary, the enforced solitude triggered the flight of imagination, a necessary condition for creative pursuits. The imposed social isolation exposed the fault lines of modern living and revealed the fragile nature of our sanity. With a constant need for human connections to maintain our mental equilibrium, the disconnect from the outer world opened up the channels to the recesses of our psyche. It was as if the lid of our subconscious was forced open to bring our repressed emotions to the fore, confronting us with our secret fears and hidden desires. This new milieu provided the perfect substrate for fabricating stories out of routine events of daily life. Plots of some of these stories bear telltale signs of the time of their birth, although many of the ideas were conceived long ago. My writing soon gained momentum and took on a life of its own beyond the lockdown, and this collection is the product of my ongoing literary journey.

I am grateful to so many people who have contributed to this book that it is impossible to name them all. The stories have undoubtedly improved from helpful feedback on their earlier drafts from many. Special thanks are due to my friends: Dr Bibhuti Pradhan, Dr Kishore Chandiramani and Dr Elamana Nandakumar for their faith in my writing; Dr Mrutyunjay Sarangi, the editor of the online magazine Literary Vibes, where these stories were first published in their previous versions and to my poet friend, Prabhanjan K Mishra, whose gentle encouragement has kept me on course in compiling this collection. I am thankful to my editor, Rachel Hall, for her meticulous attention to detail in preparing this manuscript, and to the staff at my publisher, Black Eagle Books, for giving these stories a wider audience.

Finally, I have been fortunate to receive my wife's tacit permission to indulge in my passion for writing. She has silently endured countless hours of my absence spent crafting and polishing these stories through innumerable drafts. She has also been my most sincere critic; her candid comments and quiet support sustained me through the prolonged gestation of these stories and their gradual transformation from seeds of ideas into tangible narratives. Although the stories have benefitted from the generous contributions of many, any remaining shortcomings are my sole responsibility.

Ajaya K Upadhyaya, MD
July 2024

Contents

The Visit

My visit to Ramgarh was long overdue. Since I'd left the remote village in India where I grew up until I was nine, I'd never had an occasion to return. But every time the memory of my days there sprang to mind, I would be transported to Ramgarh, thousands of miles away and a yawning gap of time ago.

Finally, after half a century, I got a chance to go on this long-awaited trip. Anticipation of what lay ahead started to build as my taxi meandered along the rural roads leading to Ramgarh. The spell of the picturesque scene of lush green paddy fields dotted with palm trees was broken only by jolts from the speed-breakers on the road, which crept up with annoying frequency.

'Anything special about this village, sir?' my driver asked.

'Yes—the house I lived in as a child!' I was unable to hide my excitement.

It was a stone bungalow where I lived with my parents when my father was the postmaster in Ramgarh. I visualised the long path from the main road to the house, which stood in the middle of extensive grounds enclosed by an imposing compound wall. A solid front gate welcomed visitors from the main road onto the dusty footpath leading to the front entrance, and a less impressive gate in the backyard led to open fields behind the house.

Rather imperiously, it stood away from the main

road as if the distance was a measure of its distinctiveness. A solid, irregular compound wall adorned the ground like a loosely fitting oversized garland. The image of a castle was more or less complete in my mind, as the space around the house was generous enough for a moat. As a child, I'd felt like a prince, secure in my castle.

My reverie was broken by the driver's next question, 'We are approaching the village now. Can you remember any landmarks for the house?'

'The house is a landmark by itself. It was the post office.'

'Nobody lives in a post office. I have never heard of such a thing.' The driver exclaimed in disbelief.

'Yes, you don't see it often. It must have been a special arrangement. It was, in fact, one of the charms of living there,' I replied.

I half-expected him to enquire more into the charm I had alluded to. But my praise for the house did not seem to make much of an impression. While I rehearsed in my mind how to phrase its charm, he fired his next question: 'How big was it?'

'It was enormous and had a spacious....'

Before I could finish, he stated, 'This is not a city; at best, it's a small town. How could it have a big post office?'

'It was the post office and the postmaster's residence, housed in one big bungalow.' Before he could interrupt me again with his questions, I continued, 'And it had a spacious garden and its own compound wall with gates in the front and the rear.' I hoped the features of the house would impress him and help him locate it.

'Sir, you now live in America. I have heard houses there are huge, like mansions. I can't imagine anything in this village to match an American house, let alone beat it in size.'

By now, the taxi had entered the village. I looked out eagerly, hoping to see something familiar. I intently scanned the road, peering into the buildings on either side for anything I could recognise.

I cast my mind back to my childhood and visualised the wide road, the vast spaces round the post office, the school building next door and the hospital further away on the other side. I pictured the bridges on the side streets branching off the main road, leading one way to the pond and the other to the mango orchard.

The excitement of seeing my childhood home after so many years kept mounting as we drove on. Soon, we came to what seemed like the end of the village, and I had not seen anything remotely familiar. The road felt cramped. The houses on both sides crowded onto the road, leaving little space for trees. It was a far cry from the image of open spaces I had carried in my mind for so long.

The unfamiliar landscape made me ask, 'Are you sure we are in Ramgarh?'

My heart sank at the driver's emphatic 'yes'.

We drove up and down the road again in the hope I'd spot something to jog my memory. While I was resigning to my failure to locate the house, we spotted a post office sign. However, a lacklustre concrete building stood behind the sign, tucked away in a neighbourhood of assorted structures. Nonetheless, we stopped.

I went inside with renewed hope to find clues to point me to my childhood home. Three clerks stood behind the counter, and I introduced myself as someone who lived in a big post office building in this village fifty years ago. My statement drew a total blank; it took a while before I received a reply.

'But the post office has always been here,' all three behind the counter replied in chorus.

'The old post office was an entirely different building—I know because I lived in it, although a long time ago,' I insisted. 'How old is this building?' I asked.

'At least twenty years, if not more.' I noted their faces appeared quite youthful, which explained their lack of knowledge of the old post office building.

After a negative reply to my question, 'Do you have anybody working here who is a bit older?' I left.

The house in my dreams couldn't have been more different from the current concrete post office. I remembered that after I'd migrated to America, I had visited the White House in Washington, DC. A friend with me on the tour commented, 'What a luxury to have one's residence and work under the same roof'.

I'd instantly replied, 'Absolutely. In fact, I was fortunate enough to enjoy that privilege as a child'. The very thought of comparing my childhood home in rural India with the White House filled my heart with pride.

Outside the post office, I looked around to see if there was anything that might help us locate the house I was after. Another landmark of Ramgarh came to me: the Maharaja's[1] palace. I remember the palace and walking through its gigantic gates into the courtyard, which was as big as a football field. I enquired with a villager on the street, who directed me down a side road. I returned to the taxi, and the driver followed the new lead. After a few minutes, we parked in front of a pair of tall gates.

The gates were shut, but one gate had a narrow opening with a hinged door towards its bottom. It was like a dog flap but bigger, just wide enough to allow visitors in, one at a time. As I squeezed myself in through this entrance, the dismal sight of the inside struck me. The buildings were in varying

---

1 *Maharaja*: king

states of disrepair, with faded paint and crumbling walls. Shrubs and trees had taken root on parts of the building. Almost all the doors were locked. In the courtyard stood an old motor car, covered in tarpaulin; it was probably out of use for ages. With no sign of human life or activity in the palace, it looked like it had been abandoned for a long time.

The palace's deserted look filled me with a mixture of sadness and curiosity. I was eager to know what happened to the Maharaja's family and how the palace had met this tragic fate.

A few visitors walked in while I was exploring. They looked young, probably in their twenties, and knew little of the palace's history. As I walked out of the palace gate, I met a man of mature years who gave me a potted history of the royal family and their palace.

'After independence, Ramgarh's Maharaja, like most royal families in India, was stripped of his royal status. The Maharajas were offered a meagre government stipend in return for their relinquished sovereignty. But Ramgarh's Maharaja was relatively well off. He had made friends in high places and astutely invested in land and property, which generated a lucrative income. He had only one son, who was sent off to the state's capital to study in a boarding school.'

As his narration proceeded, memories of the young prince came flooding into my mind. I remembered my first sighting of the prince vividly. While out in the bazaar one day with my father, a boy caught my attention. He was flanked by two men on either side, and one held an umbrella over his head. Probably no older than me, there was nothing remarkable about his looks. But, he had an air of superiority; he knew he was privileged. I had to ask my father about him and learned that he was the prince, the son of the Maharaja.

Although I did not see the prince again in the village, he remained with me for a long time. I often wondered about his life in the palace's inner chamber. I imagined him surrounded by attendants while he ate, studied, or played.

Nestled in my own castle, I felt no less than a prince. In fact, I considered myself better off. I could do whatever I wanted without any restrictions on my movements. No one would watch over me. On the other hand, the prince was escorted and chaperoned all the time. *How could he play hide-and-seek? Whom would he play with?* I'd often wondered.

'So, what went wrong then?' Pointing to the dereliction, I asked the old man, 'How did it all come to this?'

'Everything was going well when tragedy struck the royal family. One day, the boy disappeared.'

'Disappeared! But how?'

'Nobody knows what happened to him.'

'Was he kidnapped? Or murdered?'

'God only knows.'

'How can a prince just vanish? Surely, there was a police investigation. He was not a nobody; he was a prince. Didn't they find out what happened to him?'

'Of course, they tried. But extensive police investigation lasting several years showed nothing. Locally, it was big news as he was a prince, no less. The case of his dramatic disappearance remains unsolved to date.'

He paused for a moment, then continued. 'As his disappearance remained a mystery, there was no dearth of rumours: He was kidnapped and possibly trafficked or murdered by someone whom the Maharaja had slighted in some land dispute. But despite many speculations over his disappearance, nothing certain was ever established. He was never seen again and presumed dead, although there was no trace of a body.'

'More tragedy was in store for the royal family. The Maharaja was shattered. He was afflicted by a strange malady; he gave up food and stopped talking. Soon, he was reduced to a vegetable.'

'Couldn't doctors cure him? He was wealthy and well-connected. I am sure he could afford the best of medical care.'

'No expense was spared towards the Maharaja's treatment. It seemed he had lost his will to live. I think he finally died of grief.'

Didn't the royal family have relatives who could take over the palace?' I asked.

'Yes, a distant cousin came to claim it. He lived with his family in the palace for a few years but couldn't last long. They soon left, and no one has come forward to claim it or made any attempt to restore it since.'

'What went wrong?' I asked.

As the story went, the palace was haunted. The Maharaja died, and some say his spirit never left the palace. After his death, strange noises were heard from the inner chambers, and people reported ghostly shadows roaming about. The sounds and sightings were occasional at first, but as they became more frequent, the cousin found it too disturbing. He consulted astrologers and exorcists for a possible remedy, but nothing proved effective. The palace was finally abandoned many years ago.

'So, has it stood in ruins ever since?' I asked.

'Yes, as a silent witness to the tragic saga of royal might brought to its knees by cruel destiny,' he concluded.

The story of the palace was heartbreaking, but I had not forgotten the primary purpose of my trip to Ramgarh.

'You seem to know a lot about this village. Do you

have any idea about the old post office, which stood next to the school, not far from the hospital, about fifty years ago?'

'Oh yes, there was a post office, many years ago, over there,' he said, pointing to the road on which the driver and I had already driven up and down twice in our vain search.

He led us to stop by the roadside in front of a heap of stones. Between the stones and the road was a small patch of land where a couple of cows rested, chewing their cud. Behind the rubble, I noticed remnants of a few walls, their stones exposed. But the view was largely obliterated by overgrown trees.

'Is this the old post office?' I asked in utter disbelief.

'Yes, it has been abandoned for many years, too. No one has used it or lived here for a long time.'

He had no answer to my barrage of questions on how it came to be abandoned. It was clear we were at a standstill. I thanked him for his time and he went on his way.

My disappointment was instant, and it grew by the minute as I peered into the faces of the cattle resting in the foreground. The walls were barely visible through the trees. It broke my heart to see my beloved house reduced to a heap of stones. The ruins of the abandoned house reminded me of a discarded carcass left behind by vultures after they had had their fill. I secretly wished to hear that it was all a dreadful mistake, that the old post office still stood elsewhere in the village.

In the meantime, a small crowd had gathered around the car; word had spread in the village that someone from America was visiting Ramgarh in search of an old post office. I could hear them curiously chatting, looking somewhat baffled by my interest in a derelict building and the sadness on my face. But no one was able to offer me any clue to its tragic fate.

Because of the lapse of half a century, I had not expected to see the building as I'd left it. All possibilities had crossed my mind: maybe it had been remodelled, rebuilt, or—given the sheer size of the compound—developed into a block of apartments. But secretly, I had envisioned the prospect of being welcomed into the building by the present occupant after they'd learned that it had been my childhood home.

The scene in front of me was nothing like I'd imagined.

I looked at the road and the school building next to it and closely inspected the remnants of the building. A lone, waist-high broken wall with exposed jagged edges looked forlorn. Apart from the wall, there was a heap of debris, covered by thick vegetation, seemingly impenetrable. It gradually dawned on me that this was, after all, the house, I had come to see.

Much like the house, my dream lay in ruins in front of me.

I was about to return to the taxi when a man approached me. 'I hear you lived in this house as a child.' His streaks of grey hair and his confident demeanour gave him an image of authority.

Finally, I will learn something about the sad fate of my beloved house, I thought.

'Did you know this house when it was the old post office?' I asked.

'Oh yes, I remember it quite well.'

With renewed hope, I went on, 'I lived here with my parents. My father was the postmaster here, going back almost fifty years. It has been my dream to visit it again, but I never got a chance. Since migrating to America more than thirty years ago, my trips back to India were never long enough to make it to Ramgarh.'

'Ah, you left it too late,' was his sombre reply. 'I remember this house at its best; one of the fine buildings from the colonial era, a pride of Ramgarh.'

'How did it meet this dismal end?' I asked.

'It's a long story. Do you have the time for it?'

'Yes, my friend, I have waited fifty years for this visit; I shall spare no pains to at least learn what happened to it.'

'You have been out of the area so long. Do you know what happened to the Maharaja and his son?'

'I just heard of the tragic end of the Royal family. But do you know what actually happened to the young prince?'

'Yes, his life was so sad, cut short by cruel fate.'

'But what happened to him?'

'I don't know. All I know is that he was a desperately unhappy child.'

'Did you know him?'

'Yes, I met him a number of times. My father worked in the palace, and I had access to the inner chambers. We used to meet and play whenever we got a chance. But we had to be discreet, as the Maharajah disapproved of any close contact of the prince with the family of the palace staff. The prince wanted to attend the local school, like me, but his father had other ideas. Many children of his ancestors went to famous public schools far away in Dehradun or Shimla. But as the royal fortunes waned, they could not afford the expensive education they were accustomed to. As the local village school was below the status of royals, they settled for the English medium school in the nearby city.'

'I believe the prince's disappearance is still a mystery. What do you reckon happened?' My eagerness was evident in my voice.

'Who knows! Why bring up his sad story?" He looked away and quickly added, 'You were interested in the post office building, I thought'.

'Yes, but looking back, I was curious about him in those days. Of course, after leaving Ramgarh, I'd almost forgotten about him—well, until now.'

'This post office building was a part of the Royal estate, leased to the postal department as it was surplus to their needs. As their wealth dwindled, the rental income from the massive building became an important revenue stream for the Maharaja.'

'Ah, now I know how the post office building was so grand. I was really fortunate to live in it.'

'Do you want to go inside?' he asked.

'Thank you, my friend; you read my mind.' I blurted, 'I did not know we could go inside – not much is left, anyway'.

'I have been inside many times. We can go in through the rear of the building. Not many people know of the secret path.'

'Sure,' I said, unable to contain my excitement at the thought of stepping inside what remained of the edifice.

He led the way and, at the same time, kept talking. 'The prince, in fact, often spoke of the post office building—how he wished he could live in it free from the rules and restrictions of the royal household.'

As I stepped inside, I could not help taking the next turn. I faced a door frame broken down to bare stumps.

I could hear my guide's voice. 'After the disappearance of the prince and the death of the Maharaja, this building was returned to the Royal family as the postal department found the rent too high. More tenants followed. But nobody lasted long in it.'

On seeing the doorframe which led to my bedroom, I got lost in thought. The sight of the threshold of my room took me back in time, and old memories rushed in.

I remember when I lived here, I could see anything I wished at will. It was uncanny but very real. I used to spend hours lying on the bed watching scenes of my choosing, like a movie on a screen. At first, I was bemused, but it soon turned into my favourite pastime. I took it as a gift from the house, for I could not exercise my will this way when I was out of the house. Since leaving Ramgarh, I had never been able to repeat the feat.

Alongside my friends and teachers from my school, the prince figured prominently in my movies. I would see him sitting at his dining table, doing his homework, resting in his bedroom. I could turn the scenes off and on at will.

As I visualised myself sitting on my old bed, my heart raced. All of a sudden, everything changed. The whole house sprang back to life, like on a movie screen. The walls built up, stone by stone. Then, the lower part of the wall got covered by intricate patterns of *jhoti*.[2] Their white colour stood out in stark contrast with the maroon painted background, which complemented the whitewashing of the rest of the walls. My bedroom was soon complete, with my bed staring at me.

As I looked from my room beyond the corridor to the hall, more details opened up in front of me. An arched doorway, elegantly painted with decorative patterns, led from the hall into the drawing room. The drawing room was spacious; its floor displayed a pattern of checks, like a giant chess board. But its alternating colours of white and light beige had a soothing appeal.

---

2   *Jhoti*: a rural Indian art form, usually painted with fingertips, using a white paste made from rice.

The centre of this large room was dominated by a cluster of chairs around a low table. A long-armed chair occupied a corner of the large room where my father used to relax with a newspaper. In another corner stood a low stool with a clay pitcher to keep the water cool in the sweltering summers. An idol of the elephant-headed God, Ganesh, sat on a carved pedestal in another corner. The rest of the living area of the house fanned out as separate rooms from this central core. I could see their doors with decorative patterns of jhoti lining the door frames and colourful curtains with floral motifs.

Then came the verandah from the living quarters to my father's office. When I glanced to my left, the corridor to the garden spread out in front of my eyes. Next, the rugged exterior of the house was complete with its pitched tiled roof. The last thing to spring out of the ground was the entire compound wall. In no time, the property was back to as it stood fifty years ago: a cocooned castle fit for a prince.

'My heart skipped a beat. *Is this the revival of my child-hood magical power?* I was frozen as if glued to the ground.

The mystery of the prince was fresh in my mind. *How would he look now?* I wondered.

It was spooky; the image that flashed before me instantly, looked so much like my guide, who had led me into the house.

I felt faint; even breathing was difficult. With superhuman effort, I turned around to check on my friend behind me.

But I was all alone!

Next, everything else vanished- the completed grounds, the painted walls, the archways - all gone.'

Standing in the middle of the rubble, I broke into a cold sweat.

The Outsider

As soon as Alok settled in his chair, he felt an instant connection with the drawing room. He looked around, systematically examining the walls, one by one, before turning his attention to the ceiling as if searching for something. Many years had elapsed since he left this house, and he was itching to explore it. But his desire to get to know his nephews better exceeded this impulse by a wide margin. He had heard only a little of them from their father, Arun, but had never met them.

During his school years, Alok lived here in his uncle's house, along with Arun, his cousin, another nephew to his uncle. The government job of Alok's father was transferrable, so his family had to move around often. Such frequent moves proved too disruptive to his schooling. He'd been sent to live with his uncle to give his education continuity and stability.

His uncle and aunt were childless and looking for a suitable heir to pick up their mantle for posterity. At one time, Alok and Arun were contenders for the heirship of their uncle's fortune. It was common knowledge that only one would eventually bag the big prize. Not surprisingly, this injected an unspoken tension into their brotherhood, tainting their camaraderie with a sense of rivalry. At first, his uncle was grooming Alok as the heir apparent. But circumstances intervened in this scheme. Ultimately the adoption plan changed in Arun's favour, and he finally inherited their uncle's substantial estate. Subsequently, Alok had little contact with Arun; they met once or maybe twice after Alok left to pursue his college education. Since then, Arun had died somewhat prematurely, leaving the entire estate to his two sons, Prashant and Srikant, who lived in this house. And after a gap of thirty years, Alok was back at the house visiting his nephews.

***

Prashant and Srikant were utterly surprised to see their uncle out of the blue. He had landed without any notice or warning. Given the circumstances, their mutual curiosity was hard to conceal. Both brothers dropped everything to gather around their elusive uncle.

Although Prashant and Srikant had heard much from their father about Alok-uncle (as they called him), they'd never met him. They knew he'd left the country while still relatively young to study abroad before they were born. They had heard he'd settled in America. After their father's premature death, they had given up all hope of meeting their uncle. So, the visit stirred up great excitement in the household.

While Alok was in the toilet, his nephews could no longer contain their curiosity.

'What brings him here?' Prashant whispered.

'Perhaps the news of our Baba's[3] death,' Srikant said.

'But he never cared for us. He did not visit us even once when Baba was alive,'

'Maybe that makes him feel guilty,' offered Srikant.

After a few awkward moments of silence, the conversation began to flow. Prashant and Srikant had heard many stories of Alok's life from their Baba, particularly about his migration abroad. Much of what they learned did

---

3 Baba: Father in local language

not add up neatly, and some details were inconsistent, if not outright contradictory. Over the years, the picture they had of Alok-uncle, conjured up from many sources, kept changing with each new story that came their way. This only added to the mystery surrounding Alok, making their curiosity about their uncle grow.

They had little idea of the world outside Odisha. For them, its capital city, Bhubaneswar, was big enough; its wide roads and tall buildings were too imposing. They knew little about life in foreign countries, and their idea of life abroad was based on what they had seen in movies and what they heard from friends who had family members living outside India.

They busily asked Alok questions about his foray into the wider world. He tried hard to answer each query, but this was no mean task. First, he could not decide if he should be faithful to facts or remain truthful to reality. Then, he had to put everything in their mother tongue. Being away from Odisha for so many years, he had lost fluency in their mother tongue, Odia. The effort of translating into Odia what came to him naturally in English hampered the flow of conversation.

Amidst the stream of questions, the issue of money cropped up. The nephews had heard of people making vast amounts of money in America. They never knew what to believe when they heard of people in America earning *lakhs*[4] of rupees a month from menial jobs like garbage collection. This was their golden opportunity to get all their doubts cleared.

Prashant plucked up the courage to ask: 'Alok-uncle, how much do you earn in a month?'

This simple question stumped Alok. He did not mind disclosing his salary, but he stopped short of spelling out

---

4   Lakh: one hundred thousand

the figure. He was not sure what currency to put it in, dollars or rupees. A dollar figure would make little sense to them, whereas the higher figure in rupees might be viewed as a mere boast. To gain time to think it through, he threw the question back at them. 'You make a guess.'

The nephews looked lost. They were unprepared for this task.

'All right, Uncle, if you don't want to tell us, we won't force you.'

Yet their curiosity remained. 'Are you rich?' was their next question.

A straight answer to this question was again a challenge for Alok. If he said *no*, they wouldn't believe it, but the answer, *yes*, would not be entirely accurate.

He said, finally, 'I am not sure, but I am quite comfortable'. He was almost certain his answer failed to satisfy his nephews, but at least it put an end to this line of questioning.

Alok announced he was eager to visit the house, room by room, and his nephews were so happy to accompany him on the tour. He explained that every part of the house held memories; some faded, but some were still vivid in his mind. His nephews kept him company for the first few minutes of his tour. But occasionally, Alok would freeze, look at a window or a corner of a room, and seem lost in his own thoughts. They felt it was perhaps best to leave him to wander around on his own.

'Do you know why Alok-uncle never visited this house or met Baba all these years?' Srikant asked Prashant.

'How would I know?'

'I heard from Baba that Alok uncle was Badabapa's[5] favourite and was set to inherit the property.'

---

5 Badabapa: literally grandfather. Used here to address the uncle of their father

'I am not sure why he fell out of favour. Baba told me that he was not industrious enough. Hard work was not his style, and he had little respect for seniors. To top it all, he was an atheist.'

'Alok-uncle was clever,' Prashant explained, 'and his intelligence did not go unnoticed by Badabapa. But he was also lazy, spending his spare time loitering in the fields. When it came to studying, to Badabapa's annoyance, he preferred reading novels to textbooks. For Badabapa, it was wasteful to fritter away valuable time in such unproductive pursuits.'

'Was this all to disqualify him for the inheritance?'

'No, his views on a temple that Badabapa planned to erect in the village was his ultimate undoing.'

***

Alok's uncle was a fierce disciplinarian with a strong work ethic. He started life with a small holding of land and some mango groves. He grew his assets steadily, and in no time, he amassed enough land to earn the title of village landlord. With his newfound wealth, he wanted to leave a legacy. Soon, plans were afoot for erecting a temple in the village.

Alok learnt of the plans when he saw the site intended for the new temple getting cleared and dug up, ready for the laying of the temple's foundation. Soon, all his friends and teachers at school were talking about it. Alok argued at home against this extravagant project. He pointed out that there already was a temple in the village but no library. To his mind, a library would be far more useful.

But Alok was a mere schoolboy at the time. The family elders dismissed his views on the matter. In their wisdom, opening a library would fetch no *Punya (God's grace or favour)*, whereas erecting a temple would guarantee it in loads.

***

'We are lucky Alok-uncle lost the race for inheritance to this vast wealth', Srikant said.

'Yes', Prashant continued, 'I heard, Badabapa was an astute judge of character. He never made rash decisions or took impulsive actions. He was known for reserving judgment on people and taking action only after due deliberation. He was ever ready to give everyone a second or even a third chance to redeem themselves. Badabapa was prepared to overlook Alok-uncle's lack of drive and ambition. He thought it would improve with age and maturity, as Alok was still a child. But Alok-uncle's opposition to erecting the new temple was the final stroke that broke Badabapa's patience of steel. When the time came to finalise the legal heirship to the estate, our Baba won the race, as he was – in Badabapa's eyes – more deserving of this bonanza.

At the time, Alok knew his disregard for the views of seniors were hard to swallow. Soon, he realised that his irreverence in matters of God was the death knell for any remaining chance for the coveted prize of inheritance.

***

Alok had finished his tour of the house and was back in the drawing room.

'What is the name of the university, Alok-uncle? All we know is that you teach at some university in America.'

'It's called Temple University in Philadelphia, a major American city,' Alok replied.

'Temple University? But Baba told us you never liked temples.'

'It's simply a name. There is no temple; it's a university, like any other. They teach all kinds of subjects.'

'What do you teach, Alok-uncle?' Prashant asked.

'Philosophy,' he said in English. He could not come up with an Odia translation of the word.

'What is it?' Prashant persisted.

Alok struggled to find a suitable description for philosophy. In the absence of an appropriate answer, he said, 'Philosophy involves deeper study of any subject.'

Prashant added, 'We know subjects like Arts, Science, Commerce, and have heard of degrees like BA, MA, MSc, and B Com and M Com. Where does this *philosophy* come in?'

The mention of degrees was Alok's rescue line; it gave him a clue as to how to describe philosophy to his nephews. 'You see, philosophy is so deep that there is no bachelor's or master's degree. You have heard of *PhD*, haven't you?'

'Oh, yes, our college principal has a PhD. It's supposed to be the highest degree,' Srikant said.

'The full form of PhD is *Doctor of Philosophy*. The only degree in philosophy is the highest degree, a doctorate. Any subject studied in depth turns into philosophy.'

'But Baba told us that you worked in a department dealing with buildings.'

'Oh, yes – I work in the Department of Architecture. It deals with all kinds of buildings, structures, even temples,' Alok said.

'So, are you an engineer then?'

'No, I am not into building any structure. I am all thumbs when it comes to anything practical. I am interested in the purpose and meaning of buildings. I am a man of ideas, you see, not of action. I am a philosopher in the Architecture Department. My remit is harmony, beauty, and meaning of structures.'

While Alok conversed mainly in Odia so far, it was heavily interspersed with English words. He had little idea how accurately he had put his points across. He was less certain as to what his nephews made of his words. By the time he came to describe his job, he was finding it increasingly hard to translate. His last sentence, the synopsis of his job description, was entirely in English.

Prashant and Srikant gazed at Alok's face quizzically.

'We shall talk about this later. I have more important things to share with you. But I must visit the village temple before it gets too dark,' Alok said.

A surprised Srikant asked, 'The temple? Isn't that the last thing you would be interested in?'

Alok considered explaining his position on temples. He found their aesthetics immensely absorbing. His passion for temple architecture had deepened over the years, although his attitude towards the temple rituals had not altered. But he resisted this urge. He had already got them into a muddle with stories of his unconventional life, and he did not want to add any more.

As he got up, he looked straight ahead at the window on the wall leading to the adjoining room. Ah, this window and the next room held precious memories for him. He stopped to bend down and kiss the ground. As he did, the events of a night from his childhood flashed before his eyes.

***

One night, after the whole household had gone to sleep, young Alok was in the drawing room reading a book borrowed from the school library. His habit of reading storybooks was frowned upon, forcing him to read them secretly late at night. Suddenly, he heard footsteps: someone was walking towards the room. He quickly turned off the lamp and slipped the book into the next room through the window before pretending to be fast asleep. Little did he know that the next day, the room would be used as a granary for storing paddy.

Alok never saw the book again. He'd never forgotten that incident as he'd had to pay two months' pocket money towards the fine for losing the library book.

***

As Alok touched the floor, Prashant and Srikant watched, wondering, *What is he doing?*

Alok stood up quickly. Turning round towards them, he said, 'Oh, yes! I forgot to tell you. I have a present for you.' He pointed to the bag he had carried in, standing beside his chair.

'What is in it, uncle?', they asked, unable to contain their excitement.

'Ah, that is a surprise. You will have to wait until I return.' Leaving hurriedly, Alok said, 'I shall explain it later. Wait until I return. Promise you won't open it until I am back.'

Prashant walked Alok-uncle out of the house and promptly returned to the courtyard. Srikant was waiting for him there. Questions buzzed in his head, all demanding answers.

'What was Alok-uncle doing on the floor? Kissing the ground!' Srikant asked.

'This is bizarre. I am beginning to wonder if he is up to some trick', Prashant replied.

'What do you think he was doing then?'

'I remember Baba telling me the story of gold buried under the wall between this room and the room next door. During their school days, Baba and uncle were under the impression that a big chunk of the family fortune was stashed away there.' He continued, 'Did you notice, when Alok-uncle was kneeling down, he pulled out something from his pocket?'

'Yes, I saw that. It was a handkerchief.'

'But underneath the hankie, I could see something

glistening', Prashant said, taking pride in his power of observation.

'How do you mean?'

'I think he had some gadget, maybe a metal detector, to look for the buried gold', Prashant guessed.

'There is no buried gold. I never heard of any such thing,' Srikant said.

'Yes, you are right. The story of buried gold was just a rumour. But Baba told me that in their childhood, he and Alok-uncle believed in it. Perhaps for Alok-uncle, it is still real, just as he imagined in his school days.'

Srikant asked haltingly, 'So, you think he came back in search of the hidden gold?'

'Why else would he return after so many years?'

Srikant was lost in thought. He was beginning to grasp the enormity of what was unfolding. 'Bhai *(brother in local language)*, I think your hunch may be closer to the truth.'

'You saw how elusive he was, avoiding answering our simple questions. Moreover, he's been so secretive, clearly wanting to go around the house on his own to escape our scrutiny. And, what about his new interest in temples?'

Srikant's thoughts were interrupted by Prashant's next pronouncement.

"You know what? I am now worried about what is in the bag Alok-uncle has left behind."

Srikant asked, 'What are you concerned about?'

Prashant's voice had a tone of sarcasm: 'He says he has brought a present for us.'

'Don't you believe him?'

'I was unsure in the beginning. Now, I won't be surprised if this turns out to be another ploy.'

'What!' Srikant exclaimed.

'I fear the worst. You may think I am crazy, but he

may have an explosive device in it to blow us all into pieces', Prashant said in a chilling voice.

'How dare you! I cannot even imagine such a thing', Srikant shrieked.

'Well, he lost the inheritance, which he was quite certain about. He is probably back to reclaim his inheritance in another way. And, if he didn't find the gold, he might want to blow us all up, the ultimate revenge for what he perceives as a grave injustice,' Prashant said.

'So, what do we do now?' Srikant's voice was by now shrill with terror.

'We must call the police and the fire brigade. If this bag blows off, the fire brigade will come in handy, and the police should be here to gather all the evidence to nab him,' Prashant advised.

'If your instinct is right, we should first vacate the house,' cried Srikant.

No sooner had Srikant finished his sentence than they heard an explosion coming from the drawing room. They ran to the room to see what happened. To their horror, the room was ablaze. At the centre of the fire was the bag Alok-uncle had left behind. Pieces of metal and plastic were strewn all around.

They darted out of the house. After they were safely perched at a distance, Prashant took out his phone to call the police and the fire brigade.

'So, you were right after all. I did not even think this was possible,' Srikant sighed.

Then they saw Alok running towards them, flustered by the commotion generated by the fire brigade and the crowd gathered outside the house.

'Alok-uncle, here is a simple question for you. And you must tell us the truth. No more beating around the bush.

No more fobbing us with… Oh, you won't understand!' Prashant demanded.

Alok stood in utter amazement, clueless as to what Prashant was talking about.

'What was the purpose of your visit after so many years?'

Alok was speechless. He struggled to understand what had transpired and why Prashant was interrogating him. He had clearly failed to convey his sentiments for this house to his nephews.

It was now Srikant's turn to question Alok. 'Surely, you have not come here to express your condolence at Baba's death, have you?'

Alok's head was now spinning. Something had gone wrong. The brothers had got so agitated. Just an hour ago, they were in such high spirits.

Alok saw the fire brigade and firemen at work in front of the house.

'That can wait; I can explain the purpose of my visit. Tell me, first, what is the fire brigade doing here?' Alok's voice faltered.

'Now, don't pretend any more. You must come clean and confess. The police will be here soon. They will uncover your clever plot.'

'What plot? What are you talking about?' Alok cried.

'What was in that bag you cunningly left in the house before you slipped out to the temple?'

'That was your gift,' Alok said.

'You wanted to gift us an explosive? And what was your intention? To get us all killed!' he screamed.

'What? No!' As Alok looked toward the house, to his horror, he saw smoke and flames belching out of a window. Alok guessed as to what had happened. He recalled a news item from a few years ago that had warned of the danger of laptop batteries catching fire. The fire had probably come from the battery of the laptop he had brought for his nephews. He thought it was a problem of the past and that all new laptops were safe.

Before his trip, it was after considerable thought he'd decided on a laptop as a gift for his nephews. He imagined their thrill at the sight of the gift: a brand-new, top-of-its-range laptop. *How proudly they will show it off to their friends,* he'd thought at the time.

But the ultimate gift from their long-lost American uncle had gone up in smoke, literally.

'How can you even imagine such things? I brought you a laptop – the best money could buy. I thought it would make you so happy. I did not want you to open it before my return because I wanted to capture the joy on your face when you first saw it. How would I know it could catch fire?' he fumbled.

Prashant and Srikant looked at each other in total silence.

Alok slumped to the ground, sitting down with his head cupped in both hands. His face was distorted in disbelief as if he had just woken up from a horrible nightmare.

Srikant blurted out, 'How did we get it so wrong?'

'Baba once said Alok-uncle often felt no one ever understood him: He was always an outsider here.'

Prashant gulped nervously to clear his throat before saying, 'Now I can see, why.'

Divine Remedy

It was a troubling time for Doctor Prabhat Sen. A professor of Pharmacology in the Medical College, he was also the head of the department. He was a man of many talents, but research was the love of his life. However, over the last few weeks, his research had stalled.

He'd begun studying antibiotic resistance years ago when that field of research was not very fashionable, and few pharmaceutical companies were interested in promoting it. Most invested heavily in drugs to lower blood pressure and cholesterol – usually taken for years to decades – making such ventures far more profitable than exploration in antibiotics, which are generally prescribed for a week or two at best.

'You are swimming against the current,' his friends would tell him. 'Why not pursue research in areas where funding is plentiful?' But Prabhat believed in following his passion. Through years of painstaking research, he had made steady progress and was getting close to quite exciting findings.

Provisional findings from an interim study had pointed to some tantalising possibilities. These had raised his hopes for ground-breaking results, but as of yet, Prabhat's analysis had led nowhere near a conclusion. He had become stuck in the last phase and was struggling with the vast amount of data collected over the years.

As department head, Prabhat's list of responsibilities was endless. Although research was his passion, several more mundane tasks took up most of his time. Alongside his teaching duties, he had to chase procurement orders for furniture, balance the books by the end of the financial year, and discipline errant staff members. Lately, one such administrative duty had proved most vexing for Prabhat. He had to discipline Sudhakar, one of the laboratory staff for a theft from the department.

The decision to suspend Sudhakar, a trusted employees for years, had been gnawing at him. The severity of the punishment, meted out to Sudhakar, pricked Prabhat's conscience. Mental battles raging over this decision left Prabhat weary. His sapped energy and sagging concentration had slowed him down, and he had lagged behind in his research.

As his distress deepened, the research project ground to a halt. He had gathered a wealth of data and some promising original findings, which could mark the pinnacle of his research career. The glory of realising this supreme achievement, however, eluded him. It seemed he knew he was sitting on a gold mine but had no clue how to get to the gold. When it came to crunch time, his final analysis yielded frustratingly confusing results, which did not make much sense. He was at a loss to interpret or explain them.

Prabhat did not have many people in whom he could confide. There was one exception: Professor Ashok Jain, his neighbour and close friend. One would think their friendship would come in really handy for Prabhat. His problem was waning mental acuity and fading focus of mind. To address his woes, who would be better placed than Ashok, a psychiatrist?

Ashok Jain and Prabhat Sen lived in the same housing complex. But that was not all; they had much more in common. They had extensive common interests outside of medicine, and when they met, they rarely ran out of subjects for conversation.

However, they differed in one fundamental respect. Prabhat was what would be conventionally called religious, and Ashok was an atheist. Prabhat spent hours praying as his daily ritual. He would frequently bring up God's will and divine blessing in conversation, which struck Ashok as odd, almost to the point of annoyance. It amused Ashok to see Prabhat rushing into the prayer room for God's blessings before starting any important job or taking any major step.

Prabhat always carried a picture of Lord *Ganesh* (The widely revered elephant-headed God who remove obstacles and briought good luck) in his wallet. Ashok found this habit mystifying for a man steeped in science. Early in their friendship, Ashok was curious for an explanation of this strange cohabitation of science and superstition.

'Well, why do you carry a picture of your wife in your wallet?' Prabhat asked him in return.

'That's a strange question – putting people of flesh and blood in the same league as idols?'

'What is in your wallet is a mere piece of paper, but to your eyes, it represents your beloved. In the same way, Ganesh to you is simply an idol, but for me, it is a symbol of God, the Almighty.'

Over the years of their friendship, Ashok had largely given up questioning Prabhat about his orthodox beliefs and superstitious practices and would only occasionally bring it up in banter.

One evening, Prabhat was unusually quiet, which did not escape Ashok's professional eyes. It did not take Ashok long to get to what was bugging Prabhat.

Prabhat explained how he'd had to suspend Sudhakar, one of his employees in the department's animal house, for stealing animal food meant for rabbits. His discomfort with the suspension was compounded by the fact that Sudhakar's conduct was no different from that of his peers. Petty thefts of this kind were commonplace and mostly went unnoticed and unreported. Sudhakar's misfortune was that he got caught.

'You would also feel for him if you knew the full circumstances,' Prabhat continued, 'Sudhakar is basically an honest man. Everybody in the department knows I am fond of him because he is sincere and dependable. Many are jealous of him; the eyewitnesses to his theft were simply waiting for an opportunity to get him into trouble.'

'I had a private session with Sudhakar over his theft, and his explanation shocked me.' Prabhat went on, 'His salary was meagre, barely enough for his large family; a small income from his son's job supplemented it to a mere subsistence level. Since his son lost his job, his finances have been dire. First and foremost, there are so many mouths to feed. Moreover, he has to rebuild the depleted pot of savings towards his daughter's dowry. The animal food he stole from the department was to feed his hungry children.'

Before Ashok could say anything, Prabhat asked, 'Tell me honestly, have you never used department stationery, say a stapler, for personal purposes? I can't deny occasionally helping myself with a sheet of paper or a clip from my office for private work. Then, who am I to judge this lapse of Sudhakar as wrong? How is my own conduct less reprehensible than what he did?'

Ashok was struck by the comparison and the tone of remorse in Prabhat's monologue. 'You are making a mountain out of a molehill', he said by way of comforting his friend.

'How I wish I could overlook Sudhakar's theft! The amount of food he took home for his children was small; it hardly bankrupted the department's budget. But I had no choice but to take disciplinary action against him. There were witnesses to this theft, and he had already admitted to his misdemeanour. I would have been accused of favouritism if I had not suspended him; it would be a blot on my character.'

'You were simply following the rules you are bound by, Prabhat.'

There is little point in discussing more with Ashok, Prabhat thought. *He will just label me crazy and deluded.* Without uttering a word, Prabhat walked across to the prayer room. He was in search of answers to what was tormenting him the most: *How was it proper to punish Sudhakar – poor chap struggling to feed his family – by depriving him of his livelihood? It should be up to the Lord to make these difficult decisions, not mortals like me, who are nowhere near perfect.*

After Prabhat returned from prayer and resumed their conversation, Ashok finally said, 'I can see how much this is troubling you; you should better start on...,' before naming the medication.

'Thanks, but no thanks. I knew your advice before you pronounced it. This is exactly what has held me back from seeking your counsel so far.'

'But I don't understand your objection. How do you think you will overcome your...' Ashok stopped himself from completing the sentence.

'Go ahead. I also know your diagnosis of my condition from the medication you named. I am a professor of pharmacology; I can rattle off the entire classification of antidepressants. You folks are good at coining medical names for every human suffering, and your solution is always a pill of some kind,' Prabhat said. 'Can't you see human conditions in any other light?'

Brushing aside Prabhat's mocking comments, Ashok said, 'In suspending Sudhakar, you were simply doing your job. Your guilt in this matter is excessive and clearly out of proportion, which is clouding your judgement. In fact, it has disabled you to the point that you are no longer capable of doing your job.

'It isn't a sign of weakness in your character, Prabhat, that you have landed in this position,' Ashok continued. 'It is an illness, like any other, say arthritis or diabetes, for which you won't hesitate to take medication. It is not a predicament to be ashamed of; it's a condition crying out for treatment, which you must not obstruct. In fact, you should be on sick leave.'

Ashok insisted that Prabhat should at least give antidepressants a try and Prabhat reluctantly agreed. After all, how could he ignore the expert opinion? Ashok was a professor of psychiatry; his verdict was the final word on diagnosis and treatment of all things mental.

***

While the morality of Sudhakar's action might be debatable, Prabhat was in no doubt that he was wrong in disciplining Sudhakar; the sense of injustice surrounding his suspension was pushing him deeper into depression. To assuage his guilt, he offered Sudhakar money from his own pocket to tide over the crisis brought on by his suspension. But Sudhakar, grateful though he was, declined to accept it, saying he had brought this unto himself by his own actions, so he must face the consequence.

Nothing gave Prabhat much relief until he heard that Sudhakar's son, Bahadur, had managed to get a job at a construction site in the city. The building work was managed by a reputable firm, that paid its workers handsomely. The job went a long way towards easing the family's financial hardship. Prabhat's mood brightened at the news, raising his hopes that he would soon be able to complete his data analysis. But this spell of good luck was short-lived.

Disaster fell on Sudhakar's family when an earthquake struck the building site where Bahadur worked. It was not high on the Richter scale, but the epicentre was so close to the building under construction that it collapsed. Most workers managed to escape with minor injuries, but two were trapped in the rubble. Bahadur was one of them.

Rescue operations went on the whole day into the night but to no avail. The search continued the following day. By evening, there was still no sign of the missing men. The chance of finding them alive was diminishing with the passage of time, deepening the gloom in the rescue team and the anxious relatives.

Prabhat had been trying to resume his data analysis, but this grim news threw him back into despair. The results were not becoming any clearer, so he decided to return to the drawing board and look at the raw data again. He pored over the hundreds of pages of data gathered over the years.

There were plots, graphs and tables to examine. After spending hours checking each of them in minute detail, he located the master data sheet. He scrutinised it carefully, looking at it from various angles.

Suddenly the sheet brightened with a bewitching glow. Prabhat was startled and yet could not take his eyes off it. It was as if they were riveted to the glowing sheet. He shook his head, wondering what was happening to him. *Perhaps I'm overcome with fatigue and hallucinating from working such long hours.*

He looked at the graph again. The scatter plot had a number of dots. While he was focussing on the graph, something spooky happened. The contours of the dots on the graph, which were crisp to start with, first got blurred. As his attention was drawn to them, the dots started twinkling. Right in front of his eyes, they were moving. No – they were actually dancing, as if to a divine tune.

Prabhat rubbed his eyes to make sure they were not playing tricks on him. *It was for real!* The dots on the graph waltzed their way across the paper before settling down as if by an order from above. When they stopped, the plot on the graph had a new look as the dots had moved to new sites, probably where they actually belonged.

The glow faded, and the sheet was back to its old form but with a brand-new graph with an entirely different plot of dots. Prabhat realised that multiple errors had crept in when the data from previous analyses were transferred to the final graph. Although he had checked these sheets thoroughly – and more than once – somehow, he had failed to spot the errors.

Now, it became obvious that the confusing results stemmed from an oversight of his previous mistakes. As he fed the corrected set of data for analysis, results started to roll out, now crystal clear and making perfect sense. Finally, the results he had been waiting for so long were staring right at him.

Prabhat was stunned. Tears of joy rolled down his cheeks. Before doing anything, he took out his wallet, bowing his head in prayer to Lord Ganesh.

The clock in his study struck twelve, reminding him that he had been working the whole evening well into midnight. The enormity of his achievement was sinking in; Prabhat had finally, beyond all doubt, proved his theory.

***

The following morning, Prabhat was woken up with more good news. Sudhakar was at his door, with gleaming eyes and a beaming smile, to tell him of Bahadur's miraculous recovery from under the rubble. By the time he was spotted, hopes of him being found alive had faded. But there was enough of an air pocket for Bahadur to breathe. He was not only pulled out alive; he had sustained no serious injury either.

Sudhakar's good luck did not end there. The company's generous compensation policy included an *ex-gratia* payment to each worker trapped in the rubble – an eye-watering sum equal to two years of Sudhakar's salary. This grand compensation offer had initially been made for each loss of life from the disaster when the chance of finding the missing employees alive was next to nil. As a gesture of goodwill, the company decided against retrenching the offer and extended the same level of compensation, even after they were safely rescued.

This bonanza was like winning the lottery for his family. A payment of half the money was coming their way the same afternoon; the other half promised to follow within a week.

'We had given up all hope. Then, late last night, the special gadget the company had commissioned detected Bahadur's faint voice from under the rubble, saying that he was alive. It was all God's grace,' Sudhakar said.

'What was the time, you said, when Bahadur's voice was detected?' Prabhat asked.

'It was exactly midnight.'

The previous night's events flashed again in Prabhat's mind: that was also the time when he'd pulled out his wallet, making his obeisance to Lord Ganesh and saying his silent prayers.

***

That evening, when Ashok and Prabhat met, the atmosphere was jubilant. Prabhat was not sure how or what to tell Ashok about his mysterious encounter. *He won't simply believe me; even worse, he could put it down as a hallucination,* he thought. Last night's vision was best left tucked away in his own mind.

They talked at length about the implications of Prabhat's new discovery. 'This will stamp your authority in this field. You have tasted success in research before, but this is, by far, your supreme achievement. How about naming this finding after Lord *Ganesh,* the supreme remover of obstacles?' Ashok teased.

Prabhat looked at Ashok in surprise. *How could he know I prayed to Lord Ganesh late last night?* He suppressed his question and simply said, '*The Bahadur Effect* will be more apt.'

Ashok failed to grasp what Prabhat meant by his suggestion. But before questioning him about it, he said, 'I am glad you finally heeded my advice and started the medication for your depression, my friend. Usually, it takes several days to weeks to have its effect. I would not expect such a rapid response, but it may be, as you know, a placebo effect.'

'No, Ashok. Even placebos have to be swallowed to do their trick. I have a confession to make. I did not take your pill.'

'Then, what do you credit this miraculous recovery to?' Ashok asked.

'It is called *divine remedy.*'

Murder Mystery

Pratapganj, the sleepy town at the foothills of Dhauladhar Range, is accustomed to the chill of snowy weather. Its summer climate is salubrious. Tourists from all over India flock here in hordes, seeking respite from the relentless heat of the plains. The winters are mercilessly harsh, though; it is freezing cold. But a chill of a different kind had enveloped the area.

The locals were stunned by the news of a murder in Pratapganj. You could overhear people chatting, 'We did not expect this in our lifetime. It's such a peaceful place. People here have lived in harmony for generations. Burglaries and brawls are unheard of, let alone murder.'

The victim was Jaswant Lamba, a retired colonel in his seventies. He had an illustrious career in the Indian Army and had lived with his wife in Pratapganj for years. Since his wife had passed away five years earlier, he had lived alone. The Colonel had a servant, a young man, who lived in the attached servant's quarters with his family.

The Pratapganj police station was abuzz with activity. The unprecedented crime had thrown the station officer-in-charge, Samar Sharma, completely off balance. Colonel Lamba was a gentle man with no known enemy. His social circle was small, an amicable bunch of friends with no animosity whatsoever. There was no break-in, no apparent motive for the murder, and no trace of the murderer at the crime scene.

All investigations by the local police drew a blank. So, Chief Detective Inspector Arun Yadav from the head office took over the investigation. With a fresh perusal of the police file, he quickly took stock of the situation. Colonel Lamba had been shot at night, from close range, in front of his bungalow. The next morning, his body had been found lying not far from his gate. He had been alone in the house that night. His servant had gone away with his family for two days to attend a marriage ceremony in his village. A single shot had proved fatal. No firearm was found on the scene. The bungalow itself was intact, with no sign of forced entry or theft. There was no evidence of struggle or violence. Burglary was almost certainly ruled out. There was no eyewitness to the fatal shooting.

As routine enquiries failed to identify the murderer, forensic ecologist Dr Sahani was called in. Traditional detectives search for clues, such as fingerprints, fibres, hair or blood left behind by the criminal. According to Dr Sahani, criminals not only leave clues behind but also carry material from the crime scene with them, which can link them to the act. So, hoping to pin the culprit to the murder, his investigations focussed on pollens and spores unique to the crime spot.

Most people are killed by someone they know. Murder by a complete stranger is rare. The key to catching a murderer is determining the motive, which is mostly passion or revenge – unless it's a burglary gone wrong. No motive for killing the Colonel was obvious, and there was no clue to the identity of the murderer.

The people closest to the Colonel were the servant and his family, and they had not seen or heard anything unusual in the days preceding the murder. The Colonel mostly mingled with a small group of local businessmen and retired professionals. His closest friends were three couples: Rajesh Aggarwal, a vet, and his wife, Anita; Jagdish Mehra, a lawyer, and his wife, Poonam; and Dr Abhay Mahajan and his wife, Smita. Yadav decided to interview the whole lot again.

An examination of the Colonel's diary for any suspicious contact or meeting revealed no clues. His phone and message log were scrutinised for the days leading to the fateful night. Of all his calls, one stood out – Dr Abhay Mahajan's phone number. Unlike the Mehras and the Aggarwals, Dr Mahajan was a relative newcomer who had moved to Pratapganj six months ago. Seemingly a loner, he was often spotted alone on his walks, photographing the Dhauladhar Mountain range and the foothills' sprawling tea estates.

The doctor's alibi was that he spent that evening with friends at a party, and he was at home with his wife for the rest of the night. These details were corroborated by his wife and friends in their independent interviews with the police. Dr Mahajan and Colonel Lamba were acquaintances, not so close to invoke emotions strong enough for murder.

Yadav's distrust of the rigour of the local police's interrogations was not entirely without foundation. His fresh round of interviews yielded new accounts of Dr Mahajan's whereabouts that night, which simply did not add up.

At the interview with Yadav, Dr Mahajan reiterated his original statement that he'd spent the evening with the Aggarwals. Generally, he attended such parties as a couple, but intriguingly, his wife did not accompany him on that night. His explanation was that she was not in the mood to socialise.

But where was he actually that night? His friends'

statements on the time he spent at the party did not match Dr Mahajan's account. There was a discrepancy of at least an hour. So, Yadav concluded someone had to be lying about the doctor's whereabouts on the night of the murder. If the doctor was lying, what was he trying to hide? It was hard to imagine the doctor as a killer, but might he be privy to some secret that could give a clue to the motive for the murder or the identity of the murderer?

Yadav felt spurred on to dig up the doctor's background, which confirmed his suspicion that there was more to him than met the eyes.

***

After completing his psychiatry training in Delhi, Dr Mahajan settled in the nearby town of Meherpur. Although he hailed from Odisha, he quickly picked up Punjabi and became fluent in the local dialects.

As the only psychiatrist in the area, he proved immensely popular. His expertise in curing strange symptoms, which baffled local physicians because they defied anatomical explanations or had no identifiable cause, made him highly sought after. Middle-aged ladies with strange maladies, such as head-to-toe pain, young women with sudden paralysis, making housework impossible, and patients with mysterious blindness benefitted from his miraculous treatment method. Patients and their families would queue up for hours outside his clinic to ensure they would see the doctor the same day.

One fine day, he packed it all up and relocated to Pratapganj, hundreds of kilometres away from Meherpur. There was no announcement or notice about his move. What was he running away from? Was it a scandal or fallout from some professional fiasco? Could any of this be linked to the Colonel's murder?

****

Dr Mahajan was a psychiatrist. Yadav knew psychiatrists were a special breed of doctor. Their bag of tricks contains skills like hypnosis and dream interpretation to unlock the deep secrets of the mind. Psychiatric records, therefore, can provide valuable clues about a patient's worries and fears. The doctor might know the dark secrets of the Colonel's past.

Although Yadav was itching to quiz Dr Mahajan about his past, he began the interview with a gentle probe into his phone calls with the Colonel.

Was there a love triangle, an extramarital affair, or a business deal gone awry? Perhaps the Colonel had made enemies in the process, who killed him in revenge.

But the doctor had kept no records of his consultations with the Colonel.

'Did you destroy the records?'

'The question of records does not arise because Colonel Lamba was not my patient.'

'Not your patient! What were all these phone calls about, then?'

Mahajan's story was that since his retirement, he had switched his practice from psychiatry to *Positive Psychology*.

That explanation sounded too convenient. Inspector Yadav knew something about psychiatry but had never heard of this new-fangled nonsense.

'Unlike psychiatry, which deals with patients and disorders, positive psychology aims to help normal people, like you and me, to grow psychologically and be happier and more fulfilled. That is what Colonel Lamba was after. In our telephone calls, I used to guide him in mastering mindfulness practice, a meditation technique,' Dr Mahajan explained.

A bit annoyed and rather unconvinced, Yadav persevered in interrogating the doctor, hoping to unearth useful information about the murder.

'Did he talk about his worries in these sessions, or ever disclose any affair or scandal from his past, or make any mention of possible enemies? Did he ever fear for his life or feel threatened by anybody?' Yadav asked. 'That might explain his newfound interest in meditation.

'He may have mentioned worries, I suppose, but he never mentioned any threat, let alone any danger to his life.'

Inspector Yadav had pinned his hopes on the Colonel's psychiatric records. But Dr Mahajan was one tough cookie; he had answers for everything. Yadav wondered: *Is he hiding behind this mumbo-jumbo of Positive Psychology, shielding himself from links with the murder?*

As the interview was not getting anywhere, Yadav confronted Mahajan about the discrepancy in his alibi. He asked rather brusquely, 'Now, tell me the truth; where were you on the evening of the murder?'

Dr Mahajan looked worried; his forehead was covered in beads of sweat.

Is he going to collapse? Or will he come up with some trick? He is a psychiatrist, after all. Yadav considered a brief pause in the interview.

Just then, the phone rang, which provided a sound pretext for a break. Yadav asked the station staff to transfer Dr Mahajan to the next room while he attended to the phone call.

***

The caller was from the Delhi bureau. Yadav listened intently to an update on Dr Sahani's investigations and the results of his laboratory tests. He had spotted some unusual tyre marks outside the Colonel's bungalow, which were linked to a jeep registered in Delhi. His line of enquiry pointed to a contract killer who may have used this jeep for the murder. But they were still in the dark about the mastermind behind the plot.

***

By the time he was brought back to resume the interview, Dr Mahajan had regained his composure. Before Inspector Yadav could say anything, he blurted, 'I admit, I have lied. On the night of the murder, I was actually with the Mehras. But I did not want my wife to know where I spent that evening. You know, women have an overactive imagination, and my wife is no exception. She suspects Mrs. Mehra and I are having an affair.'

'Is she not right?' Yadav interjected.

'Far from it; my fondness of Mrs Mehra is entirely related to our mutual interest in Karaoke. She was the only one who would readily join me in singing duets. But, I could not convince my wife of the simple fact that Mrs. Mehra's attraction for me never extended beyond singing. For the sake of domestic peace, I told a white lie that I was spending that evening with the Aggarwals.'

'What nonsense! I have never heard such rubbish.'

'Inspector, facing a policeman's questions is an ordeal, but I am sure, even you will agree, it is nothing compared to a wife's interrogation.'

'Hmm. Your alibi for the night of the murder is now blown, so you have to come out with the whole truth. Are there more confessions to make, doctor?'

'Having lied to my wife that evening, I resolved to stick to my original story. I thought I had managed to persuade my friends to stand by my alibi. While you cops have done an excellent job in blowing my story, that does not make me a murderer.'

Inspector Yadav had been hoping to get some helpful lead, but he seemed to have turned down a blind alley. He could no longer hold himself back and turned to the story he'd uncovered.

'Dr Mahajan, tell me, what made you change your name? People do not change their names unless they have something to hide. I know your previous name was Abhishek Mohanty.'

Caught unaware by this unexpected question, Dr Mahajan fumbled for an answer.

****

The interview was again interrupted by the phone.

Inspector Yadav stepped out to take the call. The same caller from the Delhi bureau was on the line, whose voice was full of excitement. After listening for a few minutes, Yadav exclaimed, 'You mean the mystery is solved?'

'I think so. We found the driver of the jeep went into hiding, which deepened our suspicion that he was a contract killer. We eventually tracked down the jeep's owner. When the police interrogated him, he confessed to the plot of contract killing under an assignment from a rival of Colonel Lamba in Delhi. The killer drove the jeep to Pratapganj. In his hurry to get away after the shooting, he ran over the front hedge. Its pollen and spores were detected underneath the jeep, which provided the clinching evidence for the murder. The mastermind was eventually traced and cornered with all the evidence, he simply broke down.'

***

Inspector Yadav returned to the interview room. With the Colonel's murder solved, he wondered if he should bother to question the doctor anymore. But curiosity got the better of him. 'What made you change your name, doctor?' he repeated.

Dr Mahajan hesitantly replied, 'You may find it hard to believe'.

'Go on. In my career, I have heard all kinds of stories. Nothing would come as a surprise.'

'The truth is I became a victim of my own success. My clinic was attached to my residence, allowing me to devote all my time and energy to treating patients without wasting time travelling to hospitals or nursing homes.

In the beginning, I enjoyed my popularity as the only psychiatrist in the 200-kilometre radius of Meherpur. But soon, the situation spiralled out of control, and my roaring practice became a burden. When the time came for my retirement, I found it impossible to stop patients and their families from lining up outside my residence at five in the morning to see me at nine when my clinic opened.

'I desperately wanted a respite from my hectic schedule. I resorted to lying, announcing that I was away on Sundays to stop patients from gathering at my clinic so that I could spend some time at home with friends and family. But as long as I was home, patients would somehow find out and would wait outside, refusing to budge until they had had their consultation. Sometimes, I used to sneak out from the back door to escape the attention of the waiting crowd at my house, like a thief trying to evade a watchman.'

Inspector Yadav interrupted his monologue. 'So, you decided to go incognito?'

'Absolutely! It soon reached the point when my patients and their families made me a prisoner in my own home. The only way I could retire was to relocate. Quite some time ago, I had identified Pratapganj for my retirement, attracted by its weather and tranquillity. My interest in photography and my love of the mountains made Pratapganj the perfect retirement location.'

'You could have just moved away. What skeletons have you got in your closet to prompt a name change?'

'I realised simply moving away wouldn't work. Word would spread. No distance would be enough to deter patients from travelling to wherever I settled. I knew something drastic was necessary to save my sanity. I went for the unthinkable: I changed my name from Abhishek Mohanty to Ashok Mahajan so my patients could not follow me here.'

Dr Mahajan paused to ask, 'Tell me, Inspector, after devoting my entire life to healing disturbed minds, am I not entitled to some peace myself?'

Inspector Yadav chuckled. 'So, Abhishek Mohanty was murdered in cold blood by Ashok Mahajan. But that, I am sure, qualifies as mercy killing!'

A Good Life

It is hard to come up with a fitting descriptor for the life of Om Prakash. As a gardener, his life looked monotonous to casual observers, and to most, his work repetitive. For Om Prakash, however, his days were anything but dull. He couldn't remember how or when his love affair with gardening started. Working with plants had always been the most exciting thing for him, and a lifetime of gardening activity had not dimmed its charm. He had no formal qualification of any sort in horticulture or otherwise. He was entirely self-taught and honed his skills on the job. Simply put, he was a natural.

He considered himself a child of the soil and treated all plants as his kin. He was endowed with an affinity for plants, who mysteriously reciprocated his affection. To him, plants had their own character, just as people come with individual personalities. Not unlike an animal whisperer, he almost knew their language and could read their minds. Some thought he was crazy or born with an overactive imagination, bordering on pathological. Not deterred by what others thought, he was often seen in his garden, humming or singing to his plants, who in return showed off their colours and wafted their fragrance in his honour.

After years of working as a gardener, his friends and family thought Om Prakash would retire. 'People retire from boring jobs to turn to their hobbies; why would I retire when my work is so much fun?' he would say.

Despite his modest means, his children had done well in life. One son, an accountant, lived in Mumbai. By conventional standards, his second son had garnered even greater success; he became a banker and settled in Dubai. After Om Prakash's wife died, he was all alone in their house. Some of his nosy friends were curious as to why he had chosen this lonely life for himself, wondering if he had soured his relationship with his sons or, more likely, with their wives.

His sons, in fact, had never forgotten their father's contribution to their success. They would often talk of the sacrifices he had made in getting them educated. Not once, but they had offered him to live with them on many occasions.

But how little they understood their father! Om Prakash could not imagine living in Mumbai or Dubai. His son's Mumbai apartment was too cramped for him, much less his plants. His second son's house in Dubai was more spacious, but the concrete jungle of the city was a far cry from his preferred environs of greenery.

That settled the long-running debate on where Om Prakash would spend the rest of his life. For most things, time and place are two key considerations. Once the question of place was out of the way, all discussions shifted to what Om Prakash should do with his time.

Actually, the reason he turned down his children's offers ran much deeper. As his sons were growing up, their ideas began to diverge from their father's views. By the time they started work, their worlds had drifted widely apart. His sons' lives were dominated by numbers and figures. Om Prakash knew these were important, but he related much better to things he could touch and feel. His grandchildren's world drifted even further away from his, completing his sense of alienation.

He had worked all his life; the law of inertia dictated that he would continue until something intervened. But biology was knocking, too. Om Prakash was well past the retirement age; he was seventy-five. His sons offered to support him financially so he would not have to work. However, Om Prakash shrugged off all such offers, saying, 'I will die if I stop working', adding half-jokingly, 'from boredom'. Through the eighth decade of his life, his sons fought a losing battle in persuading him to stop working.

***

On his eightieth birthday, the whole family met to celebrate Om Prakash's fruitful life. His sons again pleaded with him to give up work; they said he should hang up his gardening gear and enjoy the twilight years of his life.

Om Prakash was touched. He had no doubt their concern for his welfare and comfort was genuine. Now, it was his turn to show his appreciation for their generosity. He realised he could not have everything his way all the time. As a compromise, he announced he would stop working for money, and any work he did from now on would be as a volunteer.

Om Prakash had heard of Dr Amit Trivedi's new project in the city. Dr Trivedi, a psychiatrist, had recently returned for good from America with a mission to open a hospital in India for people with Alzheimer's disease. Unlike most hospitals, services here would be completely free of charge. In fact, it was not a hospital; named *The Retreat*, it was more like a colony. It had a large garden where patients could safely and freely wander. For Om Prakash, it was a godsend. 'What better place to do voluntary work?' he thought.

He was slightly apprehensive when he went to meet Dr Trivedi to officially volunteer as a gardener in The Retreat. He knew little about the kind of patients he would encounter. Om Prakash had barely heard of Alzheimer's disease. He did not know the requirements for the job, nor did he have any idea of the doctor's expectations. While his work record contained nothing remotely adverse, he wondered if it would be impressive enough for the 'America-returned' doctor.

Om Prakash was greatly relieved to find Dr Trivedi an amiable man. He looked relatively young, perhaps in his early sixties. He had keen eyes and a disarming smile. His demeanour exuded energy and confidence. He gave Om Prakash a brief talk on Alzheimer's disease, explaining how it makes people forgetful. They gradually lose their minds and need help and care for everything in the end.

Dr Trivedi listened intently when Om Prakash recounted his gardening career and voiced a desire for voluntary work. To his delight, after getting some formalities out of the way, he was offered the gardener's post in The Retreat.

He started his new job with a degree of trepidation. His friends had warned him against working in what they viewed as effectively a lunatic asylum. Despite the reassurance from Dr Trivedi, the idea of working in a hospital for mad people was worrying; the image of them freely roaming around seemed a frightening prospect.

In the end, he was pleasantly surprised by the atmosphere at the hospital. To his great relief, he found the patients a gentle lot. Most were lost in their own worlds, almost oblivious of their surroundings, and many talked gibberish. A few hardly ever spoke as they silently pottered around as if on a mission, the purpose of which was known only to them. Call them by whatever name you like – Om Prakash found them anything but scary.

As he worked on the large garden of several acres, his appreciation for plants grew further. The giant trees on the grounds stirred a mixture of wonder and reverence in him. Walking past them was no less than a spiritual experience, like a visit to a temple. He was struck by the humility of trees like the Banyan; *it can't conceal its pride in its height, but lest it forget its humble origins as a sapling, it sends new roots down to the earth.*

Plants, he'd observed, had an amazing ability to make the most of their lot in life. Instead of moaning over what they lacked, they revelled in what they possessed. Rather than lamenting its size, the small Acer, a decorative Japanese maple, was happy to regale everyone through its daintiness. While Bougainvilleas could dazzle everyone with their bright shades of pink, jasmines stole the heart through their bewitching scent. How he wished humans could learn to be as content!

***

Over time, Om Prakash learnt a lot about Alzheimer's disease from Dr Trivedi. It creeps in stealthily, killing brain cells bit by bit, ultimately making the brain fail and rendering its victims mindless.

'Is there no treatment for this disease?'

'Yes and no. Medicines do not help much and worsen matters by their side effects. As patients tend to wander, risking accidental injury, they are treated with sedatives to slow them down. But this makes them groggy and unsteady. Powerful chemicals used to prevent them from getting lost sometimes reduce them to almost zombies. Sadly, there is no cure.'

This fuelled Om Prakash's curiosity. 'So, what do you

achieve by your treatment method, allowing them to roam around freely?'

'This, at least, keeps them happy; their quality of life is not snatched away in the name of treatment.'

Om Prakash got far more from his new venture than he bargained for. He found a kindred spirit in Dr Trivedi. Here were two people, both engaged in voluntary work, each working on something close to their hearts, driven by sheer passion.

Dr Trivedi frequently took strolls in the garden. Soon, their conversations touched on their personal lives. It turned out that Dr Trivedi was a bachelor. From the beginning, Om Prakash had been curious about Dr Trivedi's unusual mission in setting up The Retreat.

One day, when Dr Trivedi seemed to be in a friendly mood, Om Prakash asked, 'What made you return from America on this project?'

'It's a strange question, coming from you, who has himself shunned paid jobs in favour of voluntary work,'

'My situation is very different, Doctor-saab[6]. Your qualifications and experience make you almost a celebrity; you can command any fee you want. I am a mere gardener.'

'We are in the same boat, in a way. Like you, I don't have to work for a living,' Dr Trivedi said.

'What are you after, then, Doctor-saab?'

'I could have carried on working for money. But for me, all my wealth would die with me on my funeral pyre. This project is my dream; the idea of treating patients in this novel way is my brainchild. If my experiment succeeds,

---

6   Saab: a shortened version of 'sahib', which means a foreigner or a European. Its use traces back to the colonial period in India, as a suffix after the name, synonymously with 'sir' or 'master' to address people in authority as a mark of respect.

my idea will live on long after I am gone. This will be my legacy.'

Om Prakash found the conversation and concept of legacy absorbing, but it was interrupted by a phone call for Dr Trivedi. He was to meet a wealthy philanthropist who might set up an endowment for The Retreat. Soon after the call, he rushed off to a fundraising event he had organised.

***

One day, Dr Trivedi came up to Om Prakash, pointing at a gentleman coming towards him. 'Let me introduce you to our newest guest.'

Om Prakash looked at the approaching man expectantly. But he walked past them, immersed in his own world. Om Prakash barely caught a glimpse of his face.

'You will find him interesting.' Dr Trivedi added, 'His story is really sad. In the prime of his life, he was a successful businessman.'

'I thought most people who turn to charity are destitute. How did he end up here?'

'Well, he was too trusting a man. He transferred his entire business to his only son, who he believed would look after him in old age. Little did he know that his son would betray him, seize all his assets and make him virtually penniless. After his wife's death, he was left to languish alone in a rented flat. Then, he developed Alzheimer's, which made him forgetful and disorientated. He wandered out of his flat and lost his way. To his good fortune, somehow, he ended up in The Retreat.'

The condensed account of a successful but sad life was painful to hear. Still he was curious as to why Dr Trivedi thought the man would be of particular interest to Om Prakash.

'He is forgetful, and he has no idea what is wrong

with him. He can't recognise people, as his brain can't process information necessary to make sense of what he sees or hears. Sometimes, he can't even recognise himself. One day, he called the police to report an intruder in his house, as he'd failed to recognise his own image in the mirror.

'It is baffling, however, that he keeps talking to plants as if they are people.' Dr Trivedi added.

'Ah, I can see now why you thought he would interest me. What does he talk about?' Om Prakash asked.

'He remains engrossed in his own world but would stop by the plants to talk to them. It is not easy to make out, but his conversations are quite animated. Perhaps he shares his day's events with them. He seems to be telling them what to do as if they are his family or friends.'

'One day, I would decipher his talk,' Om Prakash thought.

***

The next day, he spotted the new patient from a distance. He was talking to a plant; Om Prakash could not catch the details. As he moved closer, the newcomer's face looked familiar. Still, he could not place him. A sprightly man; his gentle face, though shrunken with age and Alzheimer's disease still had a spark. His eyes were innocent yet mischievous, reminding him of his own grandson. Suddenly, it clicked. He located him in the recesses of his mind, and the floodgates of memory opened up.

'Oh, yes – he is Prem Lal Mathur; everybody called him Mathur-saab.'

Om Prakash had worked as his gardener almost forty years ago. From the constant flow of contractors and visitors into his bungalow, he guessed that Mathur-saab was into big construction projects. His supersize bungalow and its vast lawns left Om Prakash with no doubt about his extensive business and substantial wealth.

Occasionally, Mathur-saab would come up to him while he was at work in the garden all those years ago. One day, he'd caught Om Prakash singing to the plants as he watered them. Om Prakash remembered the exchange that followed when he told his surprised master that plants were no different from humans. 'They respond to music. With the right stimulation, their bloom becomes more colourful, and their fragrance more enticing.'

As he imagined Mathur-saab's face from almost forty years ago, he could no longer deny the truth. He remembered how envious he had been of Mathur-saab at the time. *He was a man with wealth, status, and a royal lifestyle. The vast garden had probably been handed to him on a plate.*

Om Prakash thought he should be ashamed of himself. *Saab had suffered so much, including the loss of his fortune and the betrayal of trust, and to cap it all, the disgrace of destitution.* Nevertheless, his face looked blissful today. The ravages of the dreadful disease failed to rob him of his inner glow.

He tried to engage Mather-Saab in a conversation but to no avail. Mathur-Saab walked away, totally oblivious to the presence of Om Prakash. Om Prakash followed him to catch his attention, but nothing worked. *I might have more success another day,* he thought.

****

On his way back home that day, Om Prakash could not take Mathur-Saab off his mind. He remembered the time when he worked for Mathur-Saab. All those years ago, Saab had been too busy a man to spare any time for gardening. Nor had he shown any interest in what Om

Prakash did, let alone any appreciation for his work. At the time, Om Prakash had no idea if he'd made an impression on Saab. But seeing him today, Om Prakash was certain: Saab had forgotten many things but not how to talk to plants. Notwithstanding his profound sadness at Saab's tragic life, this thought brought Om Prakash a modicum of comfort.

His mind next turned to Dr Trivedi and his recent conversation with him on his legacy.

Dr Trivedi has grand plans for his project; its success will keep his name alive after he is gone. No doubt, his ambitions are noble. He is no longer concerned about his own comfort; his remit is now the welfare of countless unfortunate people hit by this incurable disease. But he is still chasing achievement. He wants his name to live on beyond his death. His goalpost has moved further on, from this life to posterity.

Doctor Trivedi's face flashed in his mind as he continued walking. Lurking behind the doctor's vigour and enthusiasm were hints of anxiety, perhaps from doubts over the realisation of his dream. By contrast, Mathur-saab's face reflected picture-perfect serenity.

As he visualised Mather-Saab pottering around the garden today, he could again feel a tinge of envy welling up inside him. About forty years ago, he had envied Saab's wealth, and now he was almost becoming envious of his peace of mind.

It struck Om Prakash that if he had truly imbibed the spirit of plants, he should be least concerned about his legacy. The mere thought of legacy was disquieting; the very desire for a legacy was a sign of discontent as if a legacy would somehow make up for shortfalls in this life.

As his old memories coalesced with current events,

Om Prakash was physically shaken. It felt like he was tossed around by a rolling wave of emotions. First, he felt ashamed of his pettiness. Then, an appreciation for his good fortune rose inside him; he had lived a full life with a wealth of experience that had fallen into his lap, with little toil of his own. In the end, he was left with an overwhelming sense of gratitude towards Mathur-saab. The feeling of peace was sublime, never experienced before.

Mathur-saab had tacitly acknowledged me as his spiritual teacher and had gone well beyond paying his dues to his Guru. His payback is unconventional and most original. He is unwittingly reiterating the ultimate lesson from the world of plants, lest I forget it – the art of contentment.

His head suddenly felt light, as if a load had lifted by the flick of a switch from somewhere deep inside. As he tried to take his next step and put his foot down, he could no longer feel the ground; he was floating. He did not know where he was or what he was doing. He even forgot who he was. He also could not make out what he was seeing. It was uncanny as if the window to a new world had flung open before his eyes.

The previous day, he'd received an invitation from his sons for a grand family reunion to celebrate a religious festival on the calendar. Reading between the lines, he knew it was a disguised request for some arbitration in a family matter. *Any pearls of wisdom from me will make little sense to them.* Yet the thought of turning down their invitation pained him.

The emotional ride left Om Prakash exhausted but exhilarated. Lately, his sleep had been fitful; he had been turning on the bed frequently, interrupted by dreams too fuzzy to decipher. That night, he slept peacefully, undisturbed, like a log, never to open his eyes again.

Babas, Onions and WhatsApp

Although I have lived abroad for many years, my ties with my native India haven't weakened. They have grown somewhat stronger in proportion to my time spent out of the country, justifying the adage, 'Absence makes the heart grow fonder'. This fact has not escaped my friends, who often bring up their curiosity about India in our conversations.

One evening, when I was sharing an Indian meal with some of my British friends, one of them started talking about a glossy India Tourism advertisement he had come across. He was impressed by images of palaces, wildlife and colourful costumes, captioned: *Incredible India*.

Shrouded in mystery and mysticism, India is the cradle of one of the world's ancient civilisations. It is the home of Hinduism, the oldest religion on earth. Its heritage includes epics like the Mahabharata, the longest collection of poems ever written. Hinduism's profound philosophy has recently grabbed the world's attention, as modern physics has lent legitimacy to its ancient teachings as the essence of Truth and the ultimate metaphysical exposition of the Universe.

There are countless gurus, also known as Babas, who are the modern champions of this spiritual tradition. Their sway over the masses, irrespective of caste, creed, or class, is second only to the hold of divine authority on mortals from Indian epics.

'We have heard stories about the Babas' charisma and following. What is the secret of their success?' another friend asked.

The first friend was clearly enjoying the meal, alongside the conversation. He asked, 'Could you please pass me the curry? Its thick sauce is delicious; it has a wonderful kick to it.'

'I will come to the Babas' success in a bit', I said, acknowledging the first question. 'But let us talk about this curry first. The bulk of its delicious sauce you love is onion, generously fried in clarified butter with a blend of different spices. So, let us start with onions. Have you heard of a political party, anywhere in the world, losing elections because of high onion prices?' I asked.

My friends looked at me, surprised.

'Some years ago, the onion crop in India suffered because of erratic rainfall. A heavy monsoon destroyed the crop, leading to a severe shortage of onions, and their price shot up severalfold. Onion is a staple ingredient of Indian cooking, and the new expense annoyed the public no end. They blamed the government in power at the time for this fiasco. As a punishment for failing to curb onion prices, they voted against the ruling party when elections came. The "Onion Crisis" eventually cost them dearly; they lost the election.'

'We thought wheat and rice were the staple foods in India, like bread and potatoes in the West. We have read about the potato blight in Ireland, which caused a great famine. We have heard of the skyrocketing bread prices, which triggered the French Revolution.' My friend continued, 'But we never imagined onions played such a central role in Indian life.'

'In keeping with the global pattern, erratic rains have

become a regular feature of Indian weather, and the *Onion Crisis* returned recently. Elections in the state of Vatishgarh, a populous state, were in the offing, and the government was increasingly worried about the effect of the crisis on its popularity ratings.'

'But what has the *Onion Crisis* got to do with Babas?'

'You would not ask this question if you watched Indian news. Recently, there has been a murder attempt on a prominent minister, Mr Solanki, in Vatishgarh State. This state matters to politicians by its sheer size; the number of people in this single state exceeds the combined total population of Britain, Canada, Australia, and New Zealand. Fortunately, the murder attempt was foiled, and the alleged assailant was killed.

This sensational event has gripped the establishment, as Mr Solanki is no ordinary minister. He is one of two brothers from a well-known business family. Their father had created a vast business empire that the brothers inherited upon his death. The older brother's business flourished, but Lady Fortune did not smile so favourably on Solanki Junior.

With the liberalisation of India's economy, the nexus between politics and business became stronger. For business houses, courting financial favour in the form of licences and public contracts in return for financial aid to political parties was the modus operandi. But the junior Solanki wanted to bypass this circuitous route to power and shifted his focus straight to the ultimate target: the political chair.

His political panache proved superior to his business acumen, and he quickly rose through the ranks, becoming Second-in-command in the state cabinet. He proved his mettle recently by bringing down the price of onion in a matter of weeks, which made him a rising star in Vatishgarh politics.'

'How did he manage that?'

'The Vatishgarh government was in a real quandary over the onion crisis. They had run out of options and, in sheer desperation, were seriously considering the unthinkable: importing onions from India's arch-rival, Pakistan. Then, Solanki Junior came up with his master stroke.

His association with Baba Navjyot (literally, 'New Light') was the key to his master plan. Although India is full of gurus, Baba Navjyot belonged to a class of his own. His claim to eminence lay in reviving yoga and meditation as India's spiritual gift to the world.

'He proved to be the foremost populariser of India's ancient philosophy and traditions. His teachings charmed the public and the intelligentsia alike. His followers include film stars, politicians and luminaries from the corporate world. His promised panacea for the maladies of modern life was a return to India's roots. According to him, Ayurveda (a traditional Indian system of holistic medicine) and yoga were the twin antidotes to the toxic byproduct of our new lifestyle, known as stress.'

'But what do onion prices have to do with Babas? I thought they were after spiritual pursuits, beyond mundane concerns like the price of onion.'

'The power of Babas over people is a valuable instrument. Politicians and industrialists vie for the gurus' favour as a convenient route to influencing the masses. The Babas' hold on people has become a lucrative merchandise for sale, making some Babas very wealthy. Not long ago, one such Baba held the world record for owning the largest fleet of Rolls-Royces.'

'How does this work in the case of onion prices?'

'The price of a commodity reflects the balance between demand and supply. Onion prices shoot up when their supply goes down. The price can be manipulated down by artificially dropping the demand. The demand for most commodities depends on people's whims and fancies. This is where the hold of Babas' spirituality over the public worked wonders.

Baba Navjyot, it seems, was inducted into a scheme, whereby he wrote a blog on onion-free recipes, extolling the virtues of food cooked without onion. His blog proclaimed, "Our psyche is largely shaped by the food we eat. Onion enhances carnal desire and thus pushes us away from God".

The simple message of his recipes was: Onion-free dishes purify our soul and take us closer to God.'

'That was enough to drive down demand for onions?'

'Yes, implausible though it sounds, it worked. The message didn't just make a dent in onions' popularity – it almost killed their appeal.'

'How strange!' my friend commented. 'Food habits have developed over decades if not centuries. One would think they would be hard to shift.'

'Indeed, it is difficult to change food habits through rational argument. But we make our choices over food and drinks at an emotional level which bypasses all logic.'

'I assumed the onion scare was created out of chemicals they contain and that someone claimed they cause cancer or some such dreadful disease.'

'But in India, the wrath of God is a more powerful deterrent than the dread of disease, however serious. Currying God's favour is considered the ultimate virtue,' I said, introducing the unwavering veneration for God in the Indian psyche. 'This is where spirituality fits nicely into this plot. Invoking spirituality and bringing God into the equation charges the message with supernatural power.'

'Is there any basis to Baba's claim that onions enhance one's carnal desire?'

'Nobody knows, but facts are irrelevant here. Baba's grip on the psyche of the masses trumps any lack of scientific evidence behind the belief.'

'India is also the land of Kama Sutra', my friend interjected. 'It's amazing how easily they accepted this simplistic doctrine of earning God's favour by reducing carnal desire.'

'Who knows what the public's take on this was? In matters of sex, what is preached in public and what is practised behind closed doors are two different things.'

'But what has this got to do with the attempted murder of the Minister?' my friend asked.

'Ah, this is the most intriguing part. The investigation into the murder attempt has had no success so far. However, rumours about the mastermind behind this plot are rife. In his business and political career, the Minister had ruffled many feathers. Despite a long list of suspects, no solid evidence has emerged to pin any individual for the plot', I said, adding, 'except perhaps his own brother.'

'His own brother! What could his motive be?' my friend exclaimed.

'Under the circumstances, the key question is who had the most to lose from Solanki Junior's cunning plot? Baba's blog on onion-free recipes killed the demand for onions, and their price fell ninety per cent.'

'But wasn't everyone pleased with the falling price of onions?' my friends commented.

'Yes, the lower prices were welcomed by the public – but not the business community, who had bet on onion prices reaching record levels over the next few months. It is also no secret that the Solanki brothers had a long-standing rivalry.'

'Rivalry in families is commonplace, like competition in business, but murder is another matter.'

'Solanki Senior, an astute businessman, had accumulated huge stockpiles of onion under his control. The upward-spiralling price of onion promised him a bonanza over the next few months. But all hopes of making a fortune from this onion crisis were dashed by his brother's brainchild.'

'It seems extraordinary for a simple food blog to kill off a vegetable's appeal and make its price crash. In any case, how could the message reach the masses so quickly in a vast country like India?'

'Yes, here is the last piece of the jigsaw. It is WhatsApp. Do you know India has the world's highest number of WhatsApp users?'

'Hm, I did not know Indians were so tech-savvy. I thought illiteracy was still a problem in India!' my friend said.

'Accessing the Internet is relatively inexpensive in India, and mobile data costs a fraction of the charges we pay in the West. Moreover, illiteracy fuels the fascination with modern gadgetry and the love affair with social media. In fact, their lack of sophistication in its use makes them prime targets for propagating misinformation.'

'They must be really gullible to believe in such nonsense.'

'Well, there is a rumour floating around: Solanki Senior arranged the attempted murder of his brother through a contract killer. To deflect any suspicion of his role, however remote, in this assassination plot, the contract killer made an audacious attempt on the junior Solanki's life in full public view while both brothers were seen together.

Because the brothers looked alike, the assassin fumbled when the time came to pull the trigger. In the process, the plot was foiled, and the assassin was killed instead.'

'But, if the contract killer ended up dead in the act, what is the source of the story?'

'Exactly – but stories like this are the staple diet for circulation on WhatsApp. The public is ever ready to consume them with relish. What went on in the assassin's mind must have died with him, but that did not stop the story from spreading on social media.'

'This sounds like a plot from the films.'

'Indeed! Did you know India churns out the highest number of films in the world? But its real-life drama easily beats the most outlandish movie plot.'' I continued, 'People are ready to read and believe everything they receive on WhatsApp without pausing to think or question. More importantly, the messages on onion-free dishes from Baba Navjyot came with a stern warning in bold capitals: forward this message instantly to all your friends and family. Failure to do so will bring you unimaginable disaster.

'So, that did it?'

'Yes. It was a clever ploy to be deliberately vague about the consequences of not forwarding the message. Recipients of the messages imagined the worst misfortunes that could befall them. Like a chain reaction, the messages were repeatedly forwarded, reaching millions in a matter of minutes. And in no time, the job was done.'

'Incredible!'

Author's Note: This is a work of fiction. Although some of the events and characters in the story may resemble real-life situations, this is not meant to be a criticism of any individual, community, religion or government.

A Surgeon, a Scientist and a Shopkeeper

' Zahid sharab peene do masjid mein baith kar, ya woh jagah bataa de jahan Khuda nahin' (Allow the devout to enjoy a drink in the precinct of prayers or give them the whereabouts of the land where God does not exist). Akshay recited the Urdu couplet with gusto, lifting his wine glass.

He was savouring this drinking session with Shankar, his college friend; they were meeting for the first time after a gap of some years. It was always a treat to go down memory lane with Shankar, reliving the fun and frolic of their college days. But this was a special occasion: they were celebrating the 150th anniversary of their alma mater, Gajapati College.

Despite his sincere wishes and best efforts, Akshay had never made it to their college reunions. 'This is the price one pays for success,' he would say. He was the chief scientist, heading the neuroscience research division of an international conglomerate. From his early student days, he excelled academically. After graduating from the premier college in his native state, he'd proceeded to Delhi for post-graduate studies in physics, followed by a doctorate in neuroscience. He pursued a research career and steadily rose through the company's ranks, becoming its chief scientist. His research took him out of India early in his working life. He eventually settled in Osaka, making Japan his home.

In addition to running his own laboratory, he supervised research in several satellite sites across the globe, which kept him on his toes. His jet-set lifestyle made it virtually impossible to attend his college reunions; the dates invariably clashed with something important on his busy calendar.

He had been eagerly waiting to see many friends he'd not seen since leaving Gajapati College thirty-odd years ago. They had pursued diverse careers and dispersed across the globe. Many had risen to the top of their profession, which was hardly surprising as their college was the premier educational institute in the state. Given its impressive track record, admission into their college was highly prized; all her students were virtually guaranteed a comfortable living, no matter what they chose to do.

During college, they were ranked and grouped into types: academic, athletic, artistic, etc. Akshay had little idea what had happened to many, as he had lost contact with them. He wondered if he would even recognise them, as the passage of time must have left its mark on their looks, at least going by his own experience.

Shankar was one of his close friends from college. Over the years, they had remained in contact and met frequently. After graduation, Shankar got into medicine and made a name for himself as a renowned surgeon. Unlike many of his doctor friends who chose to emigrate, he stayed in India. He made his way through the hierarchy, becoming a professor and Head of Surgery at the local medical college.

His dexterity at wielding the scalpel was complemented by his gift for oratory and his leadership skills. He wrote extensively on medical ethics. He became the spokesperson for his fellow surgeons and enjoyed his role as an opinion-maker. Following his initial success at the state level, his influence steadily grew on the national stage. He reached his pinnacle when he became President of the National Society of Surgeons.

As Akshay chatted with Shankar, a vaguely familiar face appeared, walking towards their table. Shankar waved at him, shouting out, 'Niranjan'. As he walked towards them, Akshay had no difficulty in placing him. It was rather curious as Niranjan did not excel in sports, dramatics, or anything in particular.

Niranjan sat down and joined the conversation. Akshay gathered that Niranjan had settled locally and worked in the family business- retail shopping. Niranjan's life trajectory could not have been more different from his. After graduation, while Akshay was slogging away studying for advanced degrees, Niranjan was busy honing his business skills. Unlike Akshay, who chose an alien land thousands of miles away to call home, Niranjan hardly budged from his birthplace.

Niranjan started with his family business, which ran several grocery stores. Gradually, he expanded his business, managed supply depots, and became a wholesaler. Lately, he had acquired a retail shopping license for liquor.

The thought of Niranjan's liquor license made Akshay's body react visibly. From the corner of his eye, he saw Niranjan catching his body language. As if to hide his discomfiture, Akshay picked up his glass, saying, 'Although alcohol is much maligned, most of us do enjoy a drink'.

'Problems from excesses of alcohol are well known. It destroys lives, marriages, and families. But it is unfair to single alcohol out in this regard. There are many other things as harmful as, if not more than, alcohol. Let's pick the automobile: it kills as many people, if not more, as liquor. It damages the planet far more than alcohol. But nobody thinks it is wrong to manufacture or trade in cars or run a car showroom, Niranjan said.

'Can you really put alcohol and automobiles in the same category? Alcohol is not essential for life, whereas automobiles are clearly useful tools', said Akshay, sipping his wine.

'How useful something is depends on what we value. That turns on what enhances our enjoyment of life. Practical utility is one, but it is not the only value. There are many things of little utility that add meaning to life, such as arts and literature, which are valuable, no less, ' Niranjan replied.

'But alcohol is a toxin,' Akshay said.

'Of course – who can argue with that? However, alcohol is not the only toxin we have a love affair with. There are other examples: salt and sugar. Both, in excess, kill us, albeit slowly. As a scientist, you will agree toxins in small doses act like tonics. Who can deny that alcohol has livened up our gathering here?' countered Niranjan.

While Niranjan and Akshay discussed the morality of the alcohol business, Shankar's mind drifted. Who knew the perils of alcohol better than him? His own son developed liver failure in his thirties from heavy drinking.

The only way to save his life was a liver transplant.

The prevalent view in medical circles was to deny liver transplants to hard-core alcoholics. 'How can you waste something so precious, as the patient is bound to damage the new liver in no time from drinking?' But Shankar argued against this position on moral grounds. Social drinking is a matter of choice, a lifestyle decision, but alcoholics lose all control of their drinking. Shankar posed the question: 'How can you discriminate against alcoholics who suffer from a disease?'

His influence on medical circles was powerful enough for his wish to prevail, and he managed to get his son a liver. To everyone's relief, the operation was a success. Shankar was hopeful he could persuade his son to mend his ways. But his heavy drinking continued even after the transplant. He would drive after drinking, and one day, he was in a car accident which killed him.

Akshay said, 'I see your point. Problems with alcohol stem from excessive drinking, which is due to the drinker's lack of restraint. So, the fault lies with the drinker, not the alcohol. However, unlike salt and sugar, alcohol is not essential for life. It is an intoxicant.'

'Alcohol is not the only intoxicant. There are also drugs. We class them as dangerous; their use and supply are a crime. Why do you think alcohol is treated differently?' Niranjan asked.

Shankar replied, 'This is where money comes in. Heavy duties on alcohol make it a useful revenue stream for governments. Understandably, this source of income is too lucrative to give up.'

'I am glad you mentioned money.' Niranjan got up to refill their wine glasses. He turned towards Akshay and Shankar. In a dramatic gesture, he showed his open palms and said, 'See my clean hands; my business practice is just as clean: no adulteration. My guiding moral principle in business is this: The bottom line of any business is profit, but not at any cost.

Would you start respecting my liquor business if I say that I declare all my income diligently and pay my taxes religiously? In fact, I am the second-highest taxpayer on record in the whole state. I know many people with bigger business empires, but they pay far less tax than me; my business is puny in comparison.'

'So, you see nothing morally wrong in promoting and supplying alcohol to people who will die from its effects?' Shankar asked.

'The alternative to regulating the supply of alcohol is to ban it altogether. But we all know the paradoxical results of prohibition. Banning alcohol is like throwing out the baby with the bath water. Making alcohol illegal only benefits bootleggers and smugglers. Prohibition effectively permits criminals to print money.'

Niranjan continued, 'Supplying liquor in a regulated market is certainly a service as good as running a car dealership.'

'Really? You think running liquor shops is a service to society?'

An awkward silence followed.

With this lull in discussion, their attention turned to the music softly playing in the background. It was Jagjit Singh's[7] ghazal[8], '*Thukraao, ab ke pyaar karo, mein nashe mein hoon. Jo chaho mere yaar karo, mein nashe mein hoon*' (Whether you embrace me with love, or I resign to your rejection, I remain intoxicated).

'Without alcohol, where would you find inspiration for such soulful ghazals?' Niranjan asked.

'Alcohol is not essential for a heady sense of intoxication. As your ghazal says, love alone can elevate you to that lofty height. And so can any form of art,' Akshay said.

'But not everyone is so gifted nor so lucky. Perhaps

---

7 Jagjit Singh was a popular Indian singer nicknamed "The Emperor of Ghazals."

8 Ghazal: poem or ode to love

you will agree with me: for many less fortunate souls, alcohol remains the only path to such heights,' Niranjan asserted.

Shankar never stopped blaming the easy availability of alcohol for his son's death. But he hadn't had a chance to talk about his feelings. This conversation brought his pent-up emotions to the fore. He asked Niranjan, 'How can you sleep at night, knowing that you supply this stuff which drives decent people to the gutters? Don't the scenes of drunks lying in the gutter give you nightmares?'

'Should I be troubled by such images? They don't seem to spoil your merriment here, enjoying this lively atmosphere and sipping the stuff, which, you know, wrecks lives.'

'But is it morally right to boost personal profit through trade or supply at the expense of others' misery?' Akshay asked.

'Profit is an inherent evil of capitalism, which promotes excessive consumption. Rising consumerism deserves our condemnation in its entirety. Is it fair to single out the liquor business? How can you defend car dealers who advertise cars through slick images while berating winemakers for promoting the sale of their ware?'

Shankar wanted to move away from this discussion on alcohol and said, 'I've often wondered how wonderful it would be if we could come up with a substitute for alcohol, with all its euphoric effects but none of its toxicity'.

Now, it was Akshay's turn to talk about his research. 'This is one of my areas of research. We have been searching for this for years. It would be a boon to mankind.'

Niranjan turned towards Akshay before saying, 'This is your dharma[9], Akshay. For a scientist, your pursuit

---

9   Dharma: duty, virtue, religion, depending on the context

is knowledge. As a trader, my dharma is to maintain an effective supply chain.'

Akshay's attention level edged up a notch when Niranjan brought dharma into their conversation. Citing dharma as the bridge which linked liquor business with brain research stirred something deep inside Akshay. Perhaps it pricked his pride. In his mind, equating scientific research with running liquor shops dimmed his profession's prestige.

While Akshay was preparing for an appropriate rejoinder, Shankar piped in, 'Ah, I always wondered what "dharma" actually meant. The word dharma has been bandied about a lot, but do we really understand it?'

'Dharma, to my simple mind, means duty. It can also mean virtue, which I equate with sincerely performing my duty. I run my business with scruples, I pay my full taxes on the profits, and in the process, I provide a service to society, Niranjan replied.

'Does it not trouble you that the service you provide can potentially harm society?' Shankar asked.

'In my book, virtue lies in performing one's duty with sincerity. No action is inherently wrong. The morality of any action hinges on its motive. It's the motive which is right or wrong. The motives behind my business are manifold, but they do not include any harm to anybody.'

Akshay was unsure how to rebut Niranjan's arguments justifying the morality of his liquor business. He was still smarting from the audacious comparison and looking for a fitting reply. All he could say was, 'But you personally profit from others' misery, whatever your motives might be. How can you dress up your business as a service to society?'

Niranjan turned to Akshay: 'Your interest in your

research, I am certain, is primarily intellectual. But it is your corporate paymasters who would rake in profit from the products borne out of your painstaking work. You are a pawn on this chessboard, dominated by badshahs and wazirs[10]; they are the industrialists, patent lawyers and financiers.

Your research is a small cog in a giant wheel that moves the juggernaut of the pharmaceutical industry.'

He continued, 'We already have a happy pill, and perhaps another pill to treat boredom is on its way. What you are working on will be the next, called the euphoria capsule.'

Then, he asked, 'Your employer invests billions in your research, supporting your scientific endeavours. For them, it is a business. The primary motive of all business is profit. Does profit diminish the scientific merit of what you do?'

Akshay was unprepared for this frontal assault on his research. To deflect the discussion away from himself, he asked, 'So, Niranjan, do you consider your years spent in Gajapati College a waste of time?'

'Far from it. Those were the golden years of my life.' He continued, 'I was lucky to get into this hallowed institute. Where else could I meet talents like you all? I learnt more from you than from the teachers and textbooks put together. I was the topper in my village school, but here I mingled with gifted orators, eloquent debaters and mathematical wizards, who I never knew existed. These few years in college opened my eyes to the wider world.'

---

10 Badshah and wazir are original terms for the king and minister pieces, respectively, on a chessboard, from the Eastern world where the game of chess originated.

'Really! What was the most important lesson for you?' Shankar asked.

'The intellectual prowess of friends like you made me realise my academic limitations. But this appreciation was truly liberating. Not discouraged by this relative weakness, I was prompted to search for my strength. In fact, I found my dharma, my goal in life, on the grounds of this college.'

'How do you describe your dharma?'

'To serve the society with sincerity of purpose,' Niranjan said.

Shankar mulled over Niranjan's emphasis on sincerity of purpose. He remembered his hard battle to get his son a new liver. He was euphoric when the liver transplant operation was a success. Yet since his son's death in the car crash, doubts had crept up in his mind over his true motives.

Was he sincere in championing liver transplants for alcoholics?

Or was he just fighting for his own son's life, who was dying from liver failure, knowing well that his chances of giving up drinking were slim?

Was he being disingenuous in arguing, 'They are suffering from a disease, like diabetes or cancer? How can you deny them life-saving treatments? It's morally indefensible to write them off.'

Shankar's cherished victory in the liver transplant debate for alcoholics no longer tasted as sweet. His clever rhetoric was starting to ring hollow.

Akshay was beginning to grasp why Niranjan was instantly recognisable after so many years. As events of their college days unfolded in his mind, memories of Niranjan came alive. In their last year of college, the East Coast was devastated by a cyclone, and Niranjan volunteered for cyclone relief operations. He spent months away from his studies and had to repeat the year.

Although all students sympathised with the victims, wishing they could do something for them, their forthcoming examinations remained their primary focus. Niranjan was an exception. He was a living example of the adage: *An ounce of action is preferable to a ton of intention.* At the time, they thought Niranjan was foolish to fritter away his precious future for what seemed like a lost cause. What difference could he really make in the face of the mammoth problem?

As he looked back, Akshay's appreciation of Niranjan's efforts grew. He turned to Niranjan, 'Now I understand your mission when you joined the volunteers in the flood relief operations. While we were busy burning the midnight oil to boost our test scores, your nights were also sleepless, worrying about the safety of the stranded.'

'Yes, repeating a year was an inconvenience for me. For those affected by the cyclone and flood, it was a matter of life and death. I know my meagre contribution had a modest effect, but if it saved only one life and helped a couple of families, it made all my efforts worthwhile.

I did not mind spending an extra year catching up with all I missed during the cyclone. The degree, or my scores, for that matter, meant little to me. Examinations were important; nonetheless, all the studying done in preparation made me a more discerning person. Passing examinations or scoring well in tests was incidental.'

'Now that you are crowned the undisputed new liquor baron, Niranjan, where do you go from here?' Akshay asked.

'You mean, what will my next business be?'

Both Akshay and Shankar looked at him in anticipation.

'Remember, I am a bania[11] by birth.

Business is in my blood, and trading is in my DNA. There is bound to be some business opportunity round the corner,' he said.

'So, what is your next venture?' Shankar asked.

'Whether we like it or not, the reality is that our drinking habit is here to stay. There is a crying need for rehabilitation of alcoholics, and I don't see many good rehabilitation facilities around.'

---

11 Bania: Indian term for the social class of traders

Green Card

As he walked down the road, a big white building caught Akash's attention from a distance. As he got closer, the sign above its front door grabbed him: Reading Room. You don't see many reading rooms in this age of the Internet.

He stepped inside, not knowing what to expect. On two tables in the centre of the room were an assortment of newspapers and magazines. A few people in chairs sat around them. Akash sat down for a few moments to look at the papers on the table.

His curiosity about the Reading Room satisfied, he was about to step out. His eyes briefly landed on a young man sitting across from him. The young man stood up. Lost in his own thoughts, Akash started walking back home. As he paused briefly to avoid a stray dog running in his direction, he caught a glimpse from the corner of his eyes of the same man he'd seen in the Reading Room, now behind him. Although the young man was at a distance, Akash felt he was being followed.

He slowed down, thus closing the gap between them. Then he stopped, waiting for the young man to catch up. When he got close, Akash looked at him directly, greeting genially, 'Hello'.

'Hello,' came the reply. The young man hesitantly added, 'Where are you from, Sir? I have never seen you before.'

'You guessed it right. I am new here, visiting my brother, who lives in this town,' Akash said.

'Are you from abroad?'

'Yes. How did you guess?' Akash asked.

'Sir, it's the way you carry yourself. And you thanked the attendant of the reading room while leaving. Nobody does that here.'

They got talking, and Akash gathered that his new friend was Shashank. In no time, he was firing questions at Akash about his life, family, and work.

Akash introduced himself as a scientist living in America for many years, working as a professor of biophysics.

Shashank could not hide the real reason for his barrage of questions for long. His brother, long estranged from the family, had settled in America. He had been out of touch for many years. The family had heard nothing about him for so long that they feared the worst. Recently, though, he had contacted the family. To their surprise, he had sponsored his younger brother, Shashank, for a green card, inviting him to immigrate to America and join him.

In the beginning, Akash was puzzled by Shashank's curiosity, but now it all fell into place. Shashank was more than merely inquisitive about Akash; his interest had a clear purpose.

'That is fantastic!' Akash exclaimed, quickly adding, 'You must be mighty excited'.

'Yes, Sir', Shashank said, but his tone lacked conviction.

'America is the land of opportunities. You are free to do whatever you choose to and pursue your dreams. For a young man like you, the sky will be the limit.' Akash said.

'You are right, Sir. Everyone I have spoken to tells me the same thing. But none of them have ever visited a foreign country. Most have never been out of this state, let alone visited America. So, I don't know how much I should believe them. I doubt if they can confidently speak about America in such glowing terms.

'They might not have been out of the state or anywhere near America. But surely they know of people who have made it big in America. They have probably heard of someone who has successfully settled there.' Akash explained.

'But I want to know the reality from someone living there. I am so glad I met you. You can now see why I am bombarding you with questions.'

'I am glad, too,' Akash said, 'that I can answer your questions and clear your doubts'.

They arranged to meet again the following day at the Reading Room and strolled back, chatting about life in the USA.

By then, Shashank had learned a lot about Akash's life, including how he also grew up in a small town in India and left for the USA after his graduation. He had to study for many more years to advance his career path as a researcher and scientist. About ten years after he landed in the US, he got his coveted green card.

'Sir, do you have your green card with you?' Shashank asked. 'I want to see how it looks.'

'Sure.' Akash pulled the card from his wallet and handed it to Shashank. 'People go to enormous lengths, sometimes resorting to drastic measures, and generally wait for years to obtain one. You have been offered one on a silver plate. Just imagine how lucky you are,' Akash said.

'But I am not unhappy here in India,' Shashank replied.

'Think of the possibilities, the prospect of limitless

achievements in the USA. Whatever you can do here can be magnified severalfold in America.'

'Do you mean life is good only in America? Is it inferior everywhere else?' Shashank asked.

Akash was not prepared for such a rejoinder. Not knowing how to respond, he changed the topic. 'It seems something is troubling you.'

Shashank's phone rang, and their conversation ended as he had to leave in a hurry.

***

The next day, they met again. Akash learned more about Shashank's older brother, who had settled in the USA. He was considered a no-gooder as a child in India and was thought to lack direction and purpose. Although he was considered clever, he did not pursue education beyond graduation. His family, who had pinned their hopes on him, hoped he would study further and get a cushy government job. But he left home for Bombay, and for many years, they had no news of him until one day, out of the blue, they heard from his adopted country, America.

After they departed, Akash could not get Shashank off his mind. *The prospect of moving to a faraway land must be daunting for him,* he thought. And it's quite a leap from familiar small-town Indian life to the strange ways of the big country, America. He could feel Shashank's fear of the unknown. But something about his style of questioning suggested he was struggling with something else he had yet to declare.

***

Akash later gently enquired about the rest of Shashank's family.

Shashank's parents had died, and his grandmother was like a mother to him. With a bit of prodding, Shashank revealed what troubled him about his imminent move to the USA.

'It's my grandma I am most concerned about. She is dead against the idea of my moving to America,' he finally said.

'Why is she so set against it?' Akash asked. 'I can understand she would be anxious about how you will adjust to a foreign land so far away. But can't she see its rosy prospects?'

Shashank replied, 'Actually, her reservations strike a chord in me. I have heard strange stories about life in America.'

Shashank told the story of someone he knew who had returned from abroad after a three-year stay. He was a doctor who was quite impressed by the modern gadgets and facilities he encountered. The money was good, and all amenities were at one's fingertips. Life seemed hassle-free in America compared to the everyday irritations here.

'What was not good, then?' Akash asked, intrigued.

'The doctor worked in a hospital. When he returned to work after a week's leave, he found one of his patients still in the hospital. His ailment had been treated, and he had fully recovered. He should have been discharged while the doctor was away on leave. But it turned out the patient, an old man, lived with his daughter. She was not happy about her father coming back home.

'The doctor was curious about the reasons for his daughter's opposition to this discharge plan. "She must be a busy woman in some high-powered job, which makes it difficult for her to look after her own father. Or, perhaps, she had her own family responsibilities, which were coming in the way of her looking after her father", he thought.

'But to his surprise, he learnt that her considerations were entirely different. She had two dogs at home and didn't have the time to look after her old father, who had gone frail with age.'

Shashank paused to see Akash's reaction to this story, hoping for reassurances that it was not true.

Akash was caught off-guard by this unexpected turn in the discussion. He wanted to say that the situation was probably an exception rather than the rule.

As if Shashank could read his mind, he continued, 'Is this typical in America?'

'But she was still looking after her father instead of putting him in some old people's home. These days, even in India, it is not uncommon for people to end up in a retirement home,' Akash offered.

'It sounded like a made-up story, and I wanted to get to the truth from someone living in America,' Shashank said.

'But, looking at it from a different angle, they value all lives equally, treating pets on par with human beings. Is that a bad thing?' Akash asked. 'Family life in India is not always rosy. What about all the family feuds, some of which spill out in the open? People have been murdered in some cases,' he added.

Shashank pondered over the point Akash had made.

'Anyway, what happened in the end?' Akash asked.

'It seems home help had to be arranged for her father before she agreed to her father's discharge home.'

'So, you see, she did not send him to an old people's home. It shows she cares for her father, 'Akash said.

Shashank nodded. 'Oh, I see now; perhaps it's not that strange.'

Akash was pleased that his reasoning had not fallen on deaf ears.

As they continued their walk, Shashank thanked Akash for explaining American life in such detail. 'It has been quite a difficult decision. If I have a long chat with Grandma, I am sure I can convince her of the positive side of American life,' he told himself.

'Tomorrow is my last day here. I shall soon be returning to America, ' Akash told Shashank as they parted.

***

The following day, Akash invited Shashank for a cup of tea in the restaurant adjoining the Reading Room.

'I hope the matter is resolved and the decision made,' Akash said.

'Yes' was Shashank's brief reply.

'So, you are accepting the offer of the green card? Our next meeting will be in America!'

'No, I am not going.'

'Why not?' Akash exclaimed.

'My grandma would not budge from her view. She was greatly troubled by the prospect of my leaving for America. She went to see *Swami (a title for a Hindu ascetic or religious teacher) Uttaranand*, the renowned astrologer. People in crisis from hundreds of miles away visit him, seeking his guidance. Since her return, she has been totally opposed to the idea. No amount of reasoning can persuade her to change her mind,' Shashank said.

'But why?'

'She is convinced that if I accept this offer, she will not see me again.'

'How come?' Akash asked. 'Is it because your brother is considered a renegade, and she fears he would have a bad influence on you?'

'No. It's about what would happen to her if I went to America.'

Akash felt increasingly puzzled. 'What was the prophecy?'

'*Baba Uttaranand* told her: An important decision is looming on your horizon. Its impact on your life will be far-reaching, depending on your decision. It might take your lives to a point of no return.' Shashank paused.

Akash wondered: *So, is this the prophecy of her death?*

Akash thought of asking Shashank the age of his grandma, with a view to reasoning with him. After all, given her advanced age, this prediction should not be an impediment to this critical decision about his future. He was a young man with his whole life still ahead of him. His grandmother had already lived her life.

But the idea of discussing somebody's death made him uncomfortable. So, he tried a different tack.

'This is just a prediction, which may not come true,' he said. 'How certain is his forecast?'

'He says it's a touch-and-go case.'

'So, it isn't certain ?' Akash asked in a hopeful tone.

'But all his predictions come true. Recently my friend visited him, as he was worried about his job. He had fallen out with a colleague close to his supervisor at work. My friend feared this colleague was trying to get a black mark on his annual Confidential Report. So, he turned to *Swami Uttaranand* for some indication of what lay in store for him.'

'What was the astrologer's verdict?'

'He was absolutely correct in his prediction: "You are going through a difficult patch. You must be careful, and if you play your cards right, this crisis can be averted, but remain vigilant, as other crises are waiting in the wings for you."'

'So, what happened to him?' Akash asked.

'His supervisor had an accident and fractured both

his legs, putting him out of action for some months, and the Confidential Report was passed on to his senior officer.'

'But accidents are common. The astrologer cannot claim credit for something which could have happened purely by chance. In fact, he did not predict such a favourable outcome anyway,' Akash said.

'No, his prediction was correct! My friend was so delighted at the day's events that he went out for a drink. On returning late home that night, his wife was so incensed by his drinking that they had a mighty row.'

Akash stopped short of saying, 'Of course, such tiffs are common in couples,' because by then, he realised he had lost the argument. So instead, he continued, 'Yes, I get your point. I can see how the astrologer got it right in this instance. But do you know how many of his predictions did not come true? You simply have not heard because no one ever talks about them.'

'This debate is pointless, Sir. You seem to have a habit of questioning everything.' Shashank replied.

Just yesterday, Akash congratulated himself when he thought he had won the argument and persuaded Shashank to settle the matter logically. But faced with this unending debate around the astrologer, he knew logic was powerless.

'So, this settles the issue, and you have made your final decision on the green card?' Akash asked in a tone of resignation.

'Yes,' was Shashank's emphatic reply.

***

On their way back towards Akash's brother's house, they were caught in a drizzle while the sun was still shining, and a radiant rainbow across the sky greeted them.

Before bidding goodbye, Shashank piped up, 'Sir, do you think I have made the right decision?' as if to undo the hurt to Akash, from rejection of his advice.

'It does not matter what I think,' Akash replied, 'finding the right decision from the pack of wrong ones is difficult at best.' Looking straight ahead at the rainbow, he continued, 'It's like 'trying to pick out one colour neatly from the rest in the rainbow, at a distance, say, from here.'

The look on Shashank's face said, 'Now I don't know what you are talking about.'

Nevertheless, Akash continued, 'But it is well-nigh impossible if you attempt it when you are over there, in the middle of the rainbow'.

A strange expression flashed across Shashank's face, but Akash could not tell whether he had made his point.

Akash had thought his failure to convince Shashank might sour his mood. Surprisingly, his feeling was one of relief. He was absolved of the responsibility for Shashank's decision. Really, how did he know what would be right for Shashank? After all, Akash's own son, who had successfully settled in America, was too busy navigating his way through the maze of his job and career to spare any time for him. Although Akash and his son did not live very far apart, he could count on his fingers how many times they had met over the last ten years.

'Perhaps astrology is not all nonsense,' Akash mused. 'It probably gives the right answer, although its reasoning is absurd. Maybe it has a logic of its own.'

In a reflexive action, he pulled out his wallet and looked at his green card.

It is actually pink in colour!

Doctor's Day

There was no need to remind Dr Sitakanta Das how special the day was. It was the first of July, observed as Doctor's Day in India. It is the birthday of Dr Bidhan Chandra Roy, the legendary Indian physician whose formidable achievements spanned two diverse fields: medicine and politics. The air buzzed with greetings for doctors, but Dr Das's mind was elsewhere. The 'Happy Doctor's Day' messages from friends and well-wishers, meant to cheer him up, simply served as prickly reminders of his sticky situation.

His thoughts rolled back to his first day in medical college many years ago. His family's pride in his future prospects and his own youthful idealism made a heady mixture; he felt slightly dizzy.

Other landmarks from his long medical career flashed before him. He never forgot the day in his first year when he entered the grand dissection hall. There, cutting into the flesh of cadavers, he would learn the intricacies of human anatomy. His eyes almost smarted from the memory of the pungent formalin used to preserve dead bodies. Another memorable day was the day he started clinical medicine in his third year. Draped in a long white coat with a stethoscope around his neck for the first time, he stepped into the hospital to learn the craft of medicine from patients. Instantly, he felt quite grown-up, with a heavy sense of responsibility, as if the dangling stethoscope had infused a massive dose of maturity into him. Next, the graduation day, when he received the MBBS degree, his passport into the hallowed profession of medicine. Each milestone was deeply etched in his memory.

The college atmosphere was genial. The seniors were friendly, and the teachers were approachable. The entire setup, comprising a hostel, lecture halls, laboratory, library, and hospital wards, exuded a sense of cosiness. As he walked out with his degree, his rose-tinted view of medicine had barely prepared him for the rough and tumble of a doctor's life.

In no time, he learnt the hazards of the real world. Along the way, he also picked up necessary survival skills. The thirty-odd years of his professional journey were far from smooth. There was no shortage of challenges; some were trickier than others. These demanding situations, nonetheless, kept him engaged and alive. The excitement occasionally boiled over to frenzy; the adrenalin rush of these rare occasions added some thrill to his otherwise dull life. No encounter had been serious enough to unsettle him, let alone hinder him in his job. But everything changed on a fateful day exactly two months ago.

***

It was the first of May. Like any other day, he started his outpatient clinic. His reputation as a no-nonsense doctor with a human touch attracted patients in hordes. He ordered very few blood tests or scans, often defending his frugal practice: '*We do not treat scans or numbers on test reports; we are in the business of treating people*'. The foundation of his practice was a blend of age-old clinical wisdom and moral integrity.

While most MBBS doctors hanker after a

specialisation, Dr Das chose to remain a generalist. For him, delving into patients' stories, making sense of their confusion, and deciphering their symptoms in a vernacular they understood were the most useful tools at a doctor's disposal. *The generalist's single most valuable expertise is recognising sinister signs and symptoms that demand urgent or specialist attention. Mercifully, many illnesses are self-limiting. Doctors can cure only a handful of diseases but can always comfort patients by allaying their anxiety.*

People of all ages came streaming into his clinic for their precious few minutes with the doctor. With worried looks and eager anticipation, they would be clutching pads of papers, their entire medical records in their hands. The crowded room buzzed with activity. Despite the apparent chaos, the clinic functioned smoothly and efficiently.

A noise coming from the direction of the clinic's door rose above the room's din and disrupted the flow. There was a woman slumped in a wheelchair, pushed in by a group of people; a few were busy on their phones, and others were talking in a tone of urgency. The commotion from their animated chatter drew Dr Das's attention.

The patient was promptly transferred to the examination trolley standing in the corner of the room. Dr Das hurriedly concluded the consultation with his patient to free himself to attend to the new patient. As he was finishing his notes, he was rudely interrupted by a young man who came up to him demanding his immediate attendance to the patient on the trolley. Dr Das directed the young man to a chair in front and dutifully resumed his notes.

His concentration was broken by a scream from his assistant, Rajkishore Badajena, coming from the direction of the trolley. 'Sir, she is not breathing!'

Dr Das flung himself out of the chair and rushed to

the trolley. He immediately got down to examining the patient. As he heard no heartbeat, he started resuscitating her. Alongside his attempts to revive her, he tried to obtain details of her medical history. Despite his sustained effort at resuscitation and after giving her an adrenaline injection, there was still no sign of life. That is when he stopped to declare, 'I am sorry, she is dead.'

'What do you mean, dead!' retorted the young man.

By now, Dr Das realised that she had been brought in dead. He tried to clarify the bits of information he had gathered from different members of the group, hoping to piece them into a coherent account of how she met her tragic fate.

The young man, who seemed to be the group's spokesperson, found Dr Das's probing questions irksome. His impatience finally boiled over to anger, and he challenged Dr Das: 'Don't try to act smart, doctor. You gave her an injection and cardiac massage. You don't do that to a dead body. She was certainly alive when she arrived here in a wheelchair. Now, give us her death certificate.'

Without losing his composure, Dr Das explained that for a patient brought in dead, a post-mortem examination would be necessary for establishing the cause of death; without this, a death certificate could not be issued. His explanation made the young man angrier. He was in no mood to listen to the doctor's reasoning. Soon, they were embroiled in a heated argument over the death certificate.

Dr Das struggled to convey what happened: although the patient was brought in dead, he'd tried to revive her. But she didn't have a chance.

The young man lunged at him, landing a heavy blow on his face.

The group accompanying the dead surrounded

Dr Das, abusing him for the delay in attending to the emergency. 'Had you attended to her soon enough, she would have been saved!'

Despite the assault, he kept his calm while they reiterated their demand for her death certificate. As Dr Das was trying to figure out the real issues and get his thoughts together, he was clobbered with more blows from the group. He had little time to process what was happening.

Fortunately, Rajkishore came to his rescue. He protected Dr Das from the blows and ushered him away, diffusing the immediate tension. Pandemonium broke out in the clinic room. The patients and the accompanying family members struggled to grasp what was happening. They were left standing like dazed onlookers in a disaster zone.

A battered Dr Das was at a loss to piece together the dramatic sequence of events that had unfolded in a flash. He was relieved to find that he had sustained no serious injury but for two chipped teeth, which would require minor dental treatment. But this experience, the first of its kind in his long professional life, left him visibly shaken.

***

He was sent off duty on medical leave for a week. 'Over this time, messages from colleagues poured in, expressing outrage at the appalling violence on a faultless doctor. He learnt that the young man, the main culprit in the vicious attack, was the nephew of the state Home Minister. The rest of the gang that followed suit in manhandling him were friends of the young man and members of the deceased's family.

While Dr Das tried to make light of the event, describing his injuries as relatively trivial, his colleagues urged him to take action against what they saw as a brutal assault on the medical fraternity. The young man, the chief assailant, was known in the area for his string of misdeeds. But from the shield of protection he enjoyed through his uncle, he had rightfully earned the nickname *Mr Untouchable*. Nobody dared take any action on him for fear of reprisal. Even his cronies could get away with criminal acts of all kinds, as they, too, enjoyed the patronage of the authorities. The dire consequences of standing up against them were a powerful deterrent, sufficient to put people off taking any action.

The assault on Dr Das brought his colleagues' repressed anger and pent-up frustration to the fore. *What would be a better opportunity to nab this rogue?* A criminal conviction with a fitting sentence for his senseless attack on a doctor would teach him a lesson and send the right signal to the public.

'If you gloss over this incident, it will embolden these scoundrels and perpetuate a dangerous trend,' his friends exhorted him. 'Of course, doctors are not saints,' they said, 'and there is no lack of corrupt doctors, but Dr Das, you are the last person to deserve such ill-treatment.'

***

Dr Das was visited by his colleagues, including the chief district medical officer, generally addressed as the *Boss*, to offer sympathy for his ordeal. Sitakanta Das was an example of a vanishing breed of doctors whose professional ethics and personal integrity were exemplary. While most doctors succumb to the temptation to bend their principles, if not break them outright by normalising corrupt practices, Sitakanta was known by patients and colleagues alike to be an exception.

Dr Das asked *Boss* how best to deal with his ordeal. Going by Boss's abhorrence of the assailants' conduct. Dr Das was certain that Boss would support him if he chose to take them to court.

But *Boss* was astute enough to know that the situation was far from straightforward. 'You should be the last person to suffer this ignominy from such ruffians,' *Boss* told him. 'You have every right to press charges for this assault. You don't need my approval, let alone my permission.' He hesitated slightly before proceeding: 'In a perfect world, pursuing justice in the courts is the obvious way forward. But, here, playing your cards right will pay better dividends than standing up for principles.'

Dr Das struggled to follow *Boss*'s line of thought.

'The people you will be facing in court are well connected, with direct access to the highest offices of the state. You must not let your heart rule over your brain.'

'Should I be scared to do what is right because of the political clout of these rogues?' Dr Das asked in surprise.

'I can tell you; the minister is deeply ashamed of the misconduct of his hot-blooded nephew and his friends. He sends his apologies on their behalf.'

'But sir, accepting this abominable act lying down would send them the wrong message. All my colleagues are unanimous: they should be taken to task as a service to our profession, if not for myself.'

'The Minister is eager to compensate you handsomely for your injury and distress. He wants to know your price, whether in cash or in kind. Your cooperation will be suitably rewarded, and it will be delivered with the utmost discretion – nobody can trace any link whatsoever. I give you my personal guarantee.'

Dr Das stared at him in disbelief. *Boss should know me better; how can he even imagine I could stoop so low?*

As if *Boss* could sense Sitakanta's thoughts, he tried a different tack. Pandering to his ego, he said, 'I hope you understand where I am coming from, Sitakanta. A wise man sees opportunities in every adversity. Forgiving the wrongdoers will enhance your reputation. You will grow in stature in the public's mind.'

Dr Das's heart sank as he digested the proposal from Boss. *How does he expect me to sacrifice my principles for personal gain?* Although it was hard to dismiss his cautionary warning outright, Sitakanta's disappointment at his hypocrisy deepened as the real motive for the visit dawned on him. *Has he come here as the minister's agent to negotiate a deal for not pressing charges over the assault? Perhaps expressing sympathy was an excuse!*

Since the incident, Dr Das had been in two minds over his next move. His gut reaction was to drop the matter and move on. The injuries, after all, were not serious. Although the episode was painful, he would recover from the trauma with time. The unpleasant prospect of facing police, lawyers and court officials added to the list of cons against a court case.

But is he giving in to his base instinct of fear by not pursuing a case? What about the duty he owes to his profession? By dropping the matter, he would let his colleagues down and shirk his responsibility towards society. Ultimately, his disgust at *Boss's* proposed course of action made up his mind.

He yielded to his colleagues' demand for justice through the legal channel. *He had to stand up to the atrocious treatment of professionals in the hands of the public, who dared to assault doctors with impunity.* Counting on his flawless professional reputation, his supporters were confident that the facts of the case would favour the innocent doctor. Given the egregious violence, they doubted if the culprits, however well-connected, could escape justice.

***

The case of assault on Dr Das was duly filed with the police. The prime witness was Rajkishore, who saw the whole shocking assault from up close. The assailants would have little defence for their criminal conduct. Everyone thought it would be an open-and-shut case.

However, Dr Das came to rue the day he ceded to his colleagues' wishes. The decision triggered an unforeseen chain of events, beginning the longest nightmare of his career. Dr Das was shocked when he got arrested and taken to the police station for questioning. He faced charges under the Corruption Act for demanding money for signing a death certificate.

The allegation was that when the distressed relatives of the dead woman asked Dr Das for a death certificate, he made up a pretext of the need for an autopsy. They further alleged that his initial reluctance to issue a certificate was really a ploy for a bribe. The distressed relatives claimed they had pleaded with the doctor to reduce the bribe amount from his initial demand of Rs 50,000, but he wouldn't budge. When the family refused to pay the bribe, Dr Das became angry with them for wasting his time. In the heated stand-off that followed, the doctor pushed them. A brawl ensued that left many family members of the deceased injured.

To Dr Das's utter dismay, the family members had obtained medical certificates to support their injuries. They had also arranged eyewitnesses willing to testify in court that he was demanding money for the death certificate.

Dr Das was suspended from his job with immediate effect. Though deeply perturbed by this new development, he kept a brave face. Secure in his conviction of his innocence, he hoped the allegations against him would simply wash over. In an hour-long interview, he gave his own version of events to the police, which was totally at odds with the allegations against him.

From his naive worldview, he expected the case to proceed no further. Yet the charges against him were not dropped, and he was summoned for a court appearance. Under a new initiative to root out corruption in government posts, his case was fast-tracked, and the date for the hearing promptly arrived – the thirtieth of June.

Despite this distressing sequel, he still hoped for a full acquittal. *He had a dependable eyewitness, Rajkishore, who had seen the entire event. Surely, truth will prevail in the end,* he consoled himself. Nonetheless, the prospect of being in the dock and facing lawyers' questions was disconcerting. He kept reminding himself that he had nothing to fear as he was totally innocent, and this ghastly episode would soon be behind him. But his anger at the injustice of having to prove his innocence kept disturbing him.

Dr Das's hopes were dashed in the morning when he woke to terrible news about his key witness. Overnight, Rajkishore had suffered an accident, sustaining multiple fractures in both legs. He'd had to undergo emergency surgery, which was necessary to save his life. That morning, he was under heavy sedation and too ill to attend court and give evidence.

Dr Das's initial reaction to this grave news was concern for Rajkishore's injuries. Thankfully, his life was saved, although he was not out of danger yet. The next forty-eight hours would be critical.

As the day progressed, more news followed. Dr Das's phone was never busier; calls poured in from his friends and colleagues. More stories on Rajkishore's ghastly accident surfaced. They added up to a murky account although the details were still a mystery.

However, it was an open secret that the minister's men tried to stop Rajkishore from testifying in the corruption case against Dr Das. When that failed, they pressured him to change his account of what happened in the clinic room. They offered him bribes in exchange for withdrawing his police testimony and changing his evidence in the upcoming court hearing. When nothing seemed to work, he was threatened with dire consequences.

As neither the reward of the carrot nor the threat of the stick worked, an attack on his life was planned as the sure way to eliminate him. An accident was staged, in which he would be hit by a lorry. Fortunately, not everything went according to plan, and his life was saved. But he sustained life-changing injuries to both his legs.

Sitakanta Das had pinned his hopes on Rajkishore, whose honest testimony would clear his name. He was horrified to realise how, in his naiveté, he had overlooked the dangers to Rajkishore's life, in the process.

Dr Das was under no illusion about his own power or lack of it; his reputation was no match to the might of the minister and his cronies. Influential people in the state hierarchy were capable of ruining Rajkishore's life if he went against their wishes. He could offer Rajkishore no protection from the menacing goons and their devious ways. *Rajkishore is too loyal to me; he could not contemplate refusing to be an eyewitness in the court. It was a mistake to ask him in the first place.*

His lawyer managed to get his case adjourned by a month. *Rajkishore's testimony would no longer be his saviour.* Now, they would have to devise a new strategy for the adjourned hearing.

Sitakanta Das forced his drifting mind to focus.

After a life of dedicated service, he is suspended from his post; his crime is standing up for his principles. Although the corruption charge slapped on him is false, proving his innocence is far from simple. He has lost his prime witness with no alternative in sight; the sword of Damocles still hangs above his head. His suspension remains in effect until the case is concluded, prolonging his nightmare.

What a way to celebrate Doctor's Day!

***

As Sitakanta and his lawyer grappled with their legal quandary, a more deadly crisis was brewing in the nearby village. There had been a serious accident involving a car driven by the daughter of the Home Minister, who had knocked off a cyclist. While turning around a blind curve at speed, she did not see the oncoming cyclist. The car was travelling too fast for the curve, and as she jammed the brakes, it skidded violently, hitting a concrete wall on the roadside. Both the driver and the cyclist were flown off, landing on the road with serious head injuries.

A crowd gathered at the scene of the accident. As the identity of the car driver became known, news of the accident did not take long to reach the minister, Mr Harihar Adhikari. In no time, Sudhir Paatjoshi, his trusted right-hand man, arrived at the scene with two assistants. It became clear that both the motorist and the cyclist had sustained severe injuries and would need immediate hospital treatment.

Ordinarily, calling an ambulance to transport them to the nearby hospital would have been simple. But the COVID pandemic was raging. All the hospitals were full, leaving very few empty beds. It was difficult to get a spare ambulance to accident sites. So, the minister's men prepared to ferry the injured in their own vehicle.

But they had to locate a hospital first. They phoned

several hospitals within a fifty-mile radius. The injuries were serious, and they needed beds in the Intensive Care Unit (ICU), all of which were filled with COVID patients.

The available hospital they found had only one ICU bed, and there were two critically injured patients. Mr Paatjoshi got on the phone. Surely, some deal of some kind could be made. After all, one of the patients was the daughter of the Home Minister himself. The doctor, he proposed, could somehow conjure up an extra ICU bed.

But the man at the helm of affairs in the hospital was no ordinary doctor. He was Dr Sukumar Mahapatra, who had recently returned to India after a ten-year stint in the USA.

India has hospital chains mushrooming across its length and breadth, equipped with state-of-the-art medical technology. It is teeming with highly skilled doctors whose expertise is world-class. But most are specialists dealing with problems in the heart, brain, eyes, bones or joints. The hospitals are primarily in cities and cater to the wealthy. But what about the vast majority of Indians who live in villages? They have little choice but to rely on pitiable government hospitals with crumbling buildings, inefficient infrastructure, demoralised staff, and meagre resources.

Dr Mahapatra's dream was to fill this gap by providing quality medical care in rural India. He had opened Hospital *Suryoday* (literally meaning Sunrise), symbolising the dawn of a new era in Indian medical practice. It aimed to be a path-breaking centre, providing judicious medical care at an affordable price.

Mr Paatjoshi was losing patience with the doctor at Suryoday Hospital, who was not prepared to make any concessions. By then, the minister had arrived at the scene and personally pleaded with the doctor but to no avail. The doctor's mantra was: *Never compromise your principles because it is surely the slippery slope of corruption.* All the haggling produced only one effect: it made Dr Mahapatra more resolute in his stand.

While negotiations continued over the phone, the condition of both patients was deteriorating. The minister's daughter was getting delirious. The cyclist's consciousness was getting clouded. The thought of the minister's daughter dying under their gaze was unthinkable. And they had no idea how to deal with the injured cyclist. Desperate, they signalled each other, indicating they would ferry the minister's daughter alone and leave the cyclist behind.

A small group of men had gathered in the meantime. Too scared to ask what they were up to, they watched the minister's men closely and listened to their frantic phone calls. They made out that the sticking point was a hospital bed.

As the men walked towards the roadside to pick up the minister's daughter, a middle-aged man at the head of the pack confronted them. 'You can't simply leave him behind to die, can you?' pointing at the cyclist.

'No, we are still looking for hospital beds. We will find one soon and arrange to transport the cyclist, too.'

'We won't let you shift only one patient, leaving the other behind.'

'So far, we have located only one bed. So, let's save one of them first while we search for another bed. Why lose this bed in the meantime?' Mr Paatjoshi asked.

'But why her first?'

Mr Paatjoshi, already annoyed by the moral rectitude of the awkward doctor from the hospital, felt exasperated by the confrontation. He could feel the urge inside him to utter, *'It is the minister's order.'* But he said instead, 'She has the best chance of survival.'

'How do you know?'

Mr Paatjoshi snarled: 'How dare you question my decision? Are you a doctor?'.

'You are no doctor, either. At least I know more about medicine than you. I have worked as a compounder[12]'.

Folding his arms against his chest, with his palms joined and head bowed in mock reverence, Mr Paatjoshi ridiculed him: 'So, Doctor Saab[13], tell us then, of these two casualties, who has the best chance of survival?'

'Let Mahapatra sir be the judge of that. You must take both and let him decide,' he replied sternly.

'Really! Can you stop us?' retorted Mr Paatjoshi. Pointing at the minister in the vehicle, he said, 'Can't you see, this is the minister's order?' In a flash, the compounder laid himself flat on the ground in front of the vehicle after saying, 'Unless you take both, you have to drive over me.'

Soon, a few more men jumped forward from the pack to lay themselves on the ground, blocking the road, saying, 'See if you can drive over us to get out of this spot first.'

The compounder knew the crowd would support his actions, but he was uncertain if they were prepared to go all the way. Bolstered by this show of strength, he rose from the ground to give Mr Paatjoshi a piece of his mind. 'You have made our saint-like doctor's life hell. You have tried to kill his honest assistant because he was going to tell the truth in the court. You have got away with all your devious

---

12 Compounder: In Indian healthcare, compounders are health professionals with practical knowledge of dispensing drugs. They act as doctors' assistants in primary health centres and have seen many emergencies, accident victims, and injured people at my job.'

13 Saab: used as a suffix after peoples' names as a mark of respect. Here, it is a term of sarcasm.

plans so far. Now, you can't get out of here with her alone.'

He took a deep breath before continuing his monologue. 'If anybody has permission to play God, it is the doctor, not you or your boss. Now, let the doctor do his job without threat or bribe, for a change. Take both the injured or leave empty-handed!' And he went behind the vehicle to lay himself firmly behind its rear wheels.

The ministerial vehicle, now totally boxed in, put Harihar Adhikari and his clique in a fix, literally.

The air stood still. The ministerial flag on the car had hung its head low as if hiding its face in dejection.

Mr Adhikari looked at his bleeding daughter, lying helplessly on the roadside. He turned towards the crowd gathered in front of his vehicle. He had already contacted the deputy inspector general (DIG) of police, warning him of potential rioting at the accident site. The superintendent of police (SP) was also in the loop, keeping the reinforcement ready for action. All he needed to do was signal the SP to send the force.

Sudhir Paatjoshi could read the minister's mind and told the men lying in front of the vehicle, 'This is the minister's final order. He has made all the arrangements with the DIG of Police. The reinforcement is just a phone call away.'

Immediately, more men from the pack joined the compounder, laying themselves on the ground behind the vehicle.

Mr Paatjoshi got out of the vehicle to go round the bend and survey the state of the road beyond. He was amazed to see a jam-packed crowd. He returned to the vehicle, helplessness written all over his face. He whispered in a frightened voice, 'Sir, there is trouble ahead.'

Mr Adhikari's exasperation was reaching its peak. In

a huff, he exited the vehicle and pushed himself through the crowd while Mr Paatjoshi implored, 'Sir, sir, don't go there, please!'

Mr Adhikari was by then livid with rage and carried on regardless. But he was taken aback when he saw the huge crowd stretching as far back as his eyes could see. He wondered how so many could turn up so quickly. Alarmingly, they were armed with crowbars, sickles and swords.

The sight of weapons set his blood to boil. By the time he returned to the vehicle, his mind was made up: *Ordinary police can't control this murderous mob; only armed police will do.* He decided to phone for reinforcement from the armed police.

Before executing his deadly plan, getting the nod from the chief minister would be a good idea, he thought. Over the phone, Mr Adhikari quickly briefed the chief minister on the situation and sought his permission to deploy armed police on the rioting crowd.

'Have you gone mad!' the chief minister bellowed.

'But, sir, these people are blatantly breaking the law. It's the only option left for maintaining law and order.'

'Of course, you are the home minister, and law and order are your portfolio. But you are falling into the trap the crowd has laid for you. They are waiting for the armed police to be let loose on them. Soon, there will be a violent scuffle. Remember, self-styled social activists are waiting in the wings to publicise any police brutality in its most colourful version.'

'Sir, if I can't use the police to disperse the crowd, please give me permission to deal with this unruly mass by their own method,' he begged. 'My army of men know how to thrash them out of shape.'

'Don't make this mistake, Harihar – I implore you. These so-called champions of civil liberty will have a field day, writing about the home ministry's abuse of power and position. And, we have to be mindful of the forthcoming election.'

'What about my daughter, Sir? Her life is in real danger…' his voice trailed off.

'I share your fatherly sentiments, Harihar. But, as a public servant, you have a greater responsibility. Your duty to the people should trump your feelings for your family.'

'Sir, what do I do then?' Mr Adhikari sounded desperate.

In the meantime, the breeze had picked up momentum, setting the flag on the vehicle to flutter noisily. To the minister's ears, it was laughing aloud, mocking his impotence.

'Whatever you do, don't forget, it is the Doctor's Day today,' the chief minister said before hanging up.

To Speak or Not To

'Here is an unusual request – in fact, a favour,' Harish Chander said over the phone.

As a child specialist, I am used to receiving calls from family and friends with concerns over children's health. Harish, my friend from our college days, is now the local DSP (Deputy Superintendent of Police). His request was unusual indeed, as it was hard to categorise. Firstly, it was not about a child known to either of us. Secondly, it was not exactly a health issue. If it qualified as a health concern, it was not common, like fever, chill, vomiting or a rash. It was about Pinky, a thirteen-year-old girl from the local orphanage, Sishu Bhavan (in English, 'The Home for Children').

I visit *Sishu Bhavan* regularly to attend to the ailments of the children housed there. Over the years, I have got to know the matron, Miss Joseph, quite well. Typically, I receive a call directly from her if a situation needs urgent attention. As she had not called me about Pinky, I guessed the problem Harish was calling about was not straightforward.

'You must have heard of the fire in the warehouse in town,' Harish said by way of introduction.

I had read about the recent fire in the local news. A large *godown* (warehouse) had been burnt down; everything inside was reduced to ashes.

The godown, owned by a local businessman, had a certain notoriety. Officially a local liquor depot, it was widely rumoured to be the backbone of the supply chain for illegal drugs in the area. No one knew the value of goods that went up in flames, and the estimates varied wildly. The cause of the fire was equally unclear. Some said it was an accident, but many thought it could have been deliberate. Speculation over a motive for arson and the perpetrator's identity became fodder for gossip around town.

The mystery surrounding the fire entailed another twist. Police had apprehended two suspects from the scene, both young men, who hailed from a neighbouring village. They had been missing for a few years without any trace until police caught them fleeing from the scene of the fire.

Harish continued, 'Pinky, a young girl from *Sishu Bhavan*, ran away from the orphanage around the time of the fire and was found wandering in the area in a daze.'

'Is she all right? I hope she did not sustain any injury or suffer any burns from the conflagration.' My first concern was her safety.

'No, there are no worries of the kind. She is safe and without injury,' Harish reassured me before continuing.

'When the police picked up Pinky, they were relieved to find her alive and well. She had been registered as a missing child, and we were worried about her safety. In this day and age, we always suspect the most horrible fate for missing girls. Most are never found. By the time an alert is raised, they have been smuggled out to where they are completely out of reach of the local police. If they are ever found – it is usually their brutalised bodies.'

'So, what is the problem with Pinky?'

'She looks fine if not a hundred per cent normal. At least she is not distressed, but there is a strange look on her. She is mute; she has not uttered a word for the last 24 hours.'

'Is she fine otherwise?'

'Yes. She walks, eats and plays well; no problem at all. But she is totally mute.'

'She is probably in a state of shock. The scene of the fire may have overwhelmed her.'

'Yes, that is what we suspect. We felt we needed to allow her time to recover from her shock. But, as time has gone by, we have realised Pinky's case is bizarre.'

'Perhaps she just needs more time to recover from the trauma.'

'But there is a look on her face – it's hard to describe. You have to see her to appreciate what I am talking about. From her look, it seems she would burst out talking any minute. But she has not spoken anything. Perhaps you can make her talk.'

I was beginning to appreciate the problem Harish was struggling to convey. But my first thought was that this was a job for a specialist, well beyond my expertise. But Harish insisted I should at least have a crack at it. Child psychiatrists are not easy to find, except in metropolitan cities. Rather than continuing over the phone, I agreed to visit Sishu Bhavan and see Pinky.

***

Pinky turned out to be an ordinary-looking girl of slender build and short stature. She was dressed in a frock with large white polka dots against a red background; her hair was braided neatly in one ponytail. She had a confident gait, and her movements were brisk. If you did not know that she was mute, you would not suspect it from her demeanour. Strikingly, there was no emotion at losing the faculty of speech. Far from showing any distress, she carried on as if nothing had happened.

I gathered all that was known about Pinky's background from Miss Joseph, hoping it might give a clue to her mysterious muteness. But information on her parents or her past was scanty. Nobody could be certain of her age or where she came from. There was no missing child in her description to link her to anything. She had been picked up by police from a railway carriage, and nobody ever claimed her as a missing person. Pinky revealed little about her parents, except that she lost both of them in quick succession a few years previously. After their deaths, she stayed with a distant uncle, who never made her feel welcome in his house. One day, Pinky ran away and travelled hundreds of miles by train, mostly begging for survival. What trauma she must have endured in the process was anybody's guess. She would get so distressed talking about her life that the kindest thing seemed to be to avoid digging it up further.

Although Pinky revealed little about her own past, she took a keen interest in all the children. In contrast with her diminutive physique, she was far too advanced in her sensibility, which is rare for a child. Miss Joseph had an easy explanation for her maturity: her recorded date of birth was most likely inaccurate. Despite her sad past, her behaviour in the orphanage was surprisingly unremarkable. She rarely showed any bitterness, and her mood was always on an even keel. Moreover, there was no discernible change in her behaviour or mood leading up to her sudden disappearance on the evening of the fire.

My attempts to make Pinky talk proved futile, so I decided to try an alternative approach of communicating through pictures. I left some plain sheets of blank paper and coloured crayons with her while I discussed other issues with Miss Joseph. When I came back, I found she had scribbled something. It was unmistakably a house, with a slanted roof, a chimney, a door and two windows. Inside the house were three line drawings; they looked like two grown-ups and a child.

I returned to visit Pinky the next day to resume our pictorial communication. I was pleased to see she had added to the previous day's drawing. Streaks of red now covered the house. No amount of coaxing or cajoling yielded any lead on what she had drawn.

The following day, to my delight, she had drawn some more. There was now an outline of a bigger box-like structure around the small house, and bold smudges of red over the larger figure.

The additions to the drawing were encouraging. Pinky was communicating something; it was up to me to decipher. Although I remained hopeful, the hints were too cryptic.

***

Before my next session with Pinky, I shared my progress – or lack thereof – with Harish. Perhaps it was time to admit failure and accept that the task was beyond me. In any case, I knew at the outset that it was a job for a psychiatrist, not an average child specialist.

Harish gave me an update on the two suspects who were held in custody.

'What do the young men say about the inferno?' I asked.

'They deny any involvement in the warehouse fire and have no knowledge of who might have done it. They were simply passing by and saw nothing suspicious.'

'Are there other suspects?'

'No, but the young men's case is complicated.'

'I hear, the young men were known to have leftist leanings as college students. Since they suddenly vanished about two years ago, they are registered as missing persons. Their parents, I gather, were worried about them being groomed by a group of tribals with known links to the Naxalite[14] movement. Is there any basis for their suspicion?'

'The documents and files on the laptops in their possession are of interest to the police in their investigations into more knotty cases. Their possible role in the inferno is now eclipsed by graver concerns. The men are in custody mainly for their own protection. I can't tell you much because of the sensitivity of the issues involved.'

'I knew precisely what Harish meant by his euphemistic term - more knotty cases. It stood for a recent spate of guerrilla attacks by Naxal rebels.'

'I understand, your lips are sealed on sensitive matters. But what about the case of godown fire?'

'Not exactly, but it is no longer a major event in the eyes of the police. Fires of this kind are too common.'

'You mean the fire remains unsolved?'

'If so, it will not be the first of its kind.'

'I have been working on some clues from Pinky towards solving the puzzle of a possible arson. And I think I am getting somewhere.'

'That would be a bonus. But your main task is to make Pinky talk.'

---

14 Naxalite: An extreme Maoist group in India, considered a terrorist organisation. Originating in the 1960s, it believes in direct action, and its modus operandi is agrarian terrorism. Naxalites project themselves as the modern-day Robin Hood. Their mission is to right the wrongs of society by looting the corrupt and the rich for the benefit of the poor.

The prospect of cracking the mystery of the baffling drama was enticing, so I decided to make one more attempt.

***

I was back at the orphanage with Pinky for our last session. I looked at the drawing and could not find any change. I sat on the chair, waiting for Pinky to add something to her sketches. But she was quiet and still, seemingly in no mood to work on the drawing. *'Perhaps if she were not distracted by me, she would draw more,'* I thought.

I unfolded the newspaper and held it across my face, totally blocking me out of Pinky's view, pretending to be immersed in the newspaper. This strategy was deliberate to ensure Pinky could not see me at all. I sat, waiting, in the hope that Pinky might give more clues that would open up new avenues for exploration.

Pinky suddenly screamed, 'Sir, they did not do it!'

I was startled by her shriek and excited at once that she had finally spoken. 'What did you say, Pinky?' I asked as I folded the newspaper and put it on the table.

'They did not set fire to the godown.' She pointed at the newspaper I had just placed on the table separating us. The photo of the arrested men on the paper was staring at us.

'How do you know?'

'Because I did it.'

I scanned her face for some visible emotion when Pinky clarified, 'I set the godown on fire'.

I turned my gaze to the drawing she had worked on over the last few days. There was the small house containing the family in its centre, surrounded by a large, featureless box. The small structure looked like a family home, and the bigger one resembled a warehouse. The central figure in the drawing perched between the two adults was a child. *That must be Pinky,* I thought. It occurred to me that she drew the fire first in the family home, and next extended it to the godown.

To put my hunch to the test, I asked Pinky, 'Who is the child in your drawing?'.

She pointed a finger to herself.

I pointed at the big box-like outline of the building.

She replied, 'The godown.'

As I was mulling over my next question, she launched her monologue.

'My father was a caring man and loving father, except when he drank too much. The problem was that he was drunk most of the time. He would harass my mother, demanding money from her to buy his next drink, and beat her up when she refused. In the end, liquor killed him and destroyed our family. As a helpless young widow, she fell easy prey to the lustful eyes of the men in the locality. One day, she was found dead under suspicious circumstances. No police action followed because the police had a hand in her death. I was left an orphan. After talking to other girls, I realised I was not alone in my misfortune. Liquor has been the constant villain, wreaking havoc in the lives of so many honest, hard-working families.

'On the occasional day trips we took from Sishu Bhavan, we would sometimes go past the big godown. Someone told me it was the main liquor depot in the area. Since then, every time I passed by it I would be consumed by a rage. A desire to destroy it grew inside me, and I could not rest until I decided to burn it down.'

'Are you ready to confess to the police?'

'Yes sir, but not before these men are set free.' She pointed to the newspaper again. 'You have to believe me: they did not do it.'

'Ah! So, the photo of the arrested men was the trigger that made her talk!'

'By telling the truth to the police, you will have done your duty. Don't worry about them. If they are innocent, they will be set free anyway.'

'No, sir. You are a gentleman, and I trust you. When it comes to the police, it is a different matter. So many innocent people suffer simply because they happen to be in the wrong place at the wrong time.'

Although I was relieved she was talking, her insistence on the innocence of the suspects left me baffled.

'Who are these young men? Do you know them?'

'Sir, you are a man of influence with high connections. Otherwise, the police would not have entrusted you with this delicate task.' Sensing my scepticism, she continued, 'Take it from me, sir, they are good people. What makes you think they are guilty of anything?'

I was taken aback by her insight into the workings of police in the real world. I did not expect such perceptiveness from a child. Nonetheless, I could not work out how the men in custody fit into her version of the fire. Something was amiss with her account; there was probably more to her story than what she had disclosed so far.

Her furtive glances at the newspaper photograph continued, fuelling my suspicion that she had not told the whole truth.

'Do you know these men, Pinky? Who are they?' I repeated.

'No, I did not know them until the night of the fire. I met them for the first time at the fire scene. But I know they are good people.'

I waited for the next revelation.

'They must be set free. I have given them my word. I promised them...'

'What word? What promise did you make to them?'

'I planned it carefully. I set out that night, all prepped, to burn down the godown. That monstrous building stored the deadly poison that killed my parents and destroyed my childhood. I knew I could not rest until I did everything in my power to avenge the wrongs done to me. As I approached the godown, I saw them from afar. In the dim light, I could mark them throwing something at the godown, and it burst out in flames. In no time, it was burning furiously. The heat was fierce, and the fire blinded me.

I ran in a panic. They probably saw me, and I could hear them following me. Soon, they caught up with me. I was terrified by the thought of what they might do to me. They could have hurt me or even killed me if they wanted, but they were so decent that they were worried about my safety. They told me the godown was their enemy number one. They said they knew of countless men whose lives had been blighted by drinking. Horror stories of liquor destroying families and ruining lives were commonplace in their village. Destroying the godown was their civic duty, and they set it ablaze as a service to the public.

Everything that day had worked according to my plan. I was about to set fire to the godown, and I would have accomplished it if they had not beaten me to it by getting there first. It was as if they had read my mind and carried out my wish. As the plan was mine, I am responsible for the act, no matter who executed it.

I promised them I would take the blame for the fire. I asked them to flee the scene. What a pity, they were not fast enough. As they did it for me, I must, in return, keep my promise and confess to the police. In court, I will explain to the judge what made me go down this path. I have lost all faith in police but the judge, at least, should know better and will deliver justice.'

***

Harish phoned to congratulate me. 'My faith in your commitment to public service has been vindicated. So is my confidence in your skills.'

'I have done my bit. Now Pinky has spoken. How can you ignore her sincere appeal that the two young men should be acquitted?'

'Investigations are still ongoing. So far, they have remained tight-lipped.'

'Although they might not be entirely innocent, do you really believe that they are terrorists?'

'As I have said, fires in godowns are mostly accidental from faulty electrical connections. More importantly, there was no death or serious injury. There are no charges against these young men as yet.'

"What do you think about the outcome?' I asked.

'You know my views on the matter. I have heard your conclusion. Over the years, privately, we have despaired at the ravages of illicit drugs in our society. And, our conclusion has been unanimous: Our judiciary is hopelessly inadequate in tackling the drugs menace.'

As I put the phone down, I wondered: What would I do if I were asked to speak for Pinky or the young men in court?

Would I rather not talk at all because I would not know where to begin?

The Consummate Confidant

'Is something bothering you?' My friend, Anupam, asked.

He had astutely read my mind. We were en route to our college reunion, seated comfortably inside Anupam's plush car, perhaps luxurious by some standards. He took evident pride in his recent acquisition and its latest gadgets. He'd paused after a short lecture on the car's technical specifications.

We have been friends since our college days. It was easy for Anupam to sense my lack of excitement.

'I did not want to interrupt your flow. Of course, this is a nice car.'

'But, it is not just your lukewarm interest in my car. You have been rather quiet from the moment we got inside.'

'Yes, I'm tired, perhaps from my long flight. It is jet lag, I guess.'

Although our lives had taken different routes and followed divergent trajectories, we had remained in touch. He stayed in India while I went abroad. I'd initially gone for a brief stint but eventually settled in America. College reunions would bring us together regularly, but the pandemic and the lockdown put a stop to our routine meetings, and we had not met for about three years.

Anupam had always been curious about the Western lifestyle and the secret of its attractions that pull people away from their motherland. He would often say, 'It can't be a simple matter of money. With your skill set, you can make as much, if not more, money in India. Arguably, your life would be more comfortable here.' He would ask me about my social circle, enquiring about my friends, particularly those without an Indian background. He would often quiz me on how I formed friendships with the locals and what common interests did bind us.

He made no secret of his fascination with the peculiarities of life in the West. Their hobbies struck him as weird. For example, he couldn't grasp how watching birds and insects could be an exciting pursuit. *One must be crazy to enjoy sitting idly, holding a fishing rod for an entire day.* He would ask me how I spent my leisure hours and what I did for entertainment. He would be inquisitive about our topics of conversation and the songs or jokes we enjoyed in social gatherings.

On this ride, he continued exploring his favourite field of enquiry. I did not mind giving him my perspective in general terms but, I was not comfortable naming people or recounting their lives. Something would hold me back. The reason for my hesitation became obvious to me when we stopped for a cup of coffee.

As we sat down with our coffees, I realised I needed the privacy to feel free to talk. In the car, the driver's presence inhibited my flow.

'I must come clean, Anupam. I told you a white lie when I said I was too tired to chat.'

'What!'

'Yes, the real reason was different; it was your driver, Paresh.'

'But what did he do? He has been my most trustworthy and reliable driver. That is why I sent him to pick you up from the airport.'

'Oh no – he did nothing wrong.'

'Then, how did he stop you from talking?'

'It is simply his presence in the car.'

Anupam gave me a puzzled look as if I had uttered something preposterous.

I realised my statement was too opaque. *I owed him a more explicit explanation.* But first, I had to certify Paresh's driving skill and testify to his conduct, which was beyond reproach.

'You have a very able driver in Paresh. The problem lies with me, not with him.'

'Now, you have been confusing me even more. If he is a capable and courteous driver, what is your problem?'

'Anupam, he did a sterling job in receiving me at the airport.'

'Now, stop talking in riddles.'

'Let me start at the beginning. Unlike you in India, I am not used to being chauffeured around. I drive my own car, and when riding with friends or family, there is no stranger in the car. I have got so accustomed to the privacy of riding without a chauffeur that the presence of an outsider hampers conversations about personal matters. Your luxury of being driven around comes at a price - the imposition of this outsider.'

'But drivers do not join our conversation unless we invite them to.'

'Even if they don't participate, they can hear you…'

'So, what?'

'Well, some things are best contained amongst close friends or family. Don't you agree?'

'Ah! Are you worried about drivers passing on your secrets to others?'

'What they actually do is not the point. But the mere

possibility is enough to hamper open exchange in their presence.'

'Now, I know what is troubling you. It seems you believe in everything you read in novels or see in movies.'

'What novel are you talking about? Which movie?'

'I have not read the book, but I have seen the movie based on the novel. The book got some sort of award. I thought you would know.'

'Oh yes. You are talking about The White Tiger[15].'

'Yes, that story is about a murderer who happened to be a driver. But he is one of a rare breed of rogue drivers, far from the average.'

'I am glad you have seen the movie. We can at least talk about it. What did you make of the plot?'

'Well, it is an amusing story. But it is fiction. In real life, Indian drivers are loyal and certainly not killers. Most drivers become part of the family. You must not tarnish all drivers in the same brush because one of them turns out to be a murderer.'

'Of course, not every Indian driver murders their master. I agree everything is dramatised in fiction to make a point. The murder of one's own master, I admit, is rare, but murdering their confidentiality is a staple game for most drivers. They must be boasting in their circle of drivers, regaling them of all the secrets in their master's household.'

'A real outsider might be tempted to do that. But the driver is hardly an outsider.'

---

15 The White Tiger by Arvind Adiga (2008) is a Booker Prize-winning novel. It illustrates the stark contrast in material wealth in Indian society, where grinding poverty and flagrant opulence coexist. The novel's central character is a clever driver who, to escape poverty, resorts to murdering his master when he realises he can get away with it.

'Too many personal matters divulged in private exchanges are best kept out of public knowledge. It may be unintentional, but what about drivers inadvertently passing them on to others?'

'Now, I see the real problem. Your obsession with privacy is making you paranoid. Like everything in life, a bit of privacy is a good idea, but too much can be toxic. You in the civilised West boast of your progressive thinking. But your preoccupation with confidentiality is morbid, making you a prisoner in your private world. You miss out on the simple joys of mingling with others and all the fun of gossip. No wonder it has made you an emotional recluse.'

'But you go to the other extreme and trivialise confidentiality as if privacy is a dirty word!'

Before I could make my point, Anupam interrupted: 'What is it you wanted to say anyway? Paresh is not here; so, can we talk now?'

In our close circle of friends, we have a common friend, Gagan, a confirmed bachelor. Over the years, we have teased him endlessly about what he was missing out by his choice of bachelorhood. He would shrug off our banter with his favourite line, 'Marriage best suits the mediocre.' The rest of us, all married friends, would quote statistics of how married men live longer, and he would rebut these, saying, 'Longer perhaps, but not necessarily happier'. We used to taunt him with quotes in favour of marriage: 'By all means, marry. If you get a good wife, you'll become happy; if you get a bad one, you'll become a philosopher.' He would laugh it off, saying, 'Look at some of the greatest human achievements globally. Many of them are bachelors. You don't have to be a genius to figure out why. You can pursue your passion and follow your goals without distraction or interference from the yoke of marriage'.

I did not dare mention Gagan's name while we were in the car. We had an outsider in the car, who I thought, must be kept out of Gagan's private life. I could not wait to hear about Gagan's latest amorous adventure. I asked, 'What is Gagan up to these days?

'Oh yes, there are steamy stories about his romantic escapades. Have you not heard of his recent fling with someone half his age?'

'I heard about an affair. But you call it a fling. Confirmed bachelors are not immune to the trap of feminine charms. There is no shortage of examples of such avowed advocates against marriage falling for a femme fatale late in life.'

'He has been too possessive of his personal life lately. We rarely see him in public.'

'I suppose you could ask his driver.'

'No chance; his driver is not a character from Adiga's novel. Anyway, Gagan is attending the reunion. Why don't you ask him directly?'

It was time for us to return to the car to resume our journey. Paresh greeted us with his customary courtesy. As I sat in the car, the conversation we had over coffee about drivers was fresh in my mind. Paresh certainly did not have a profile of a murderer; he looked too meek for that. *But would he betray someone's confidence and spill the beans?* There was no way of judging that.

***

I remembered my first meeting with Paresh when he drove me from the airport. As we got into the car, he asked if he should play music on the car's stereo system. I found his politeness refreshing as, in my experience, most drivers turn it on without asking. To break the ice between us, I'd started with general enquiries into his background.

His parents had migrated from a village to the state's capital city. His father had a basic schooling, and getting a job in the village was out of the question. Without much land to speak of, he subsisted on working as a labourer. Making ends meet was a challenge in the village. But life in the city was not much easier. Jobs were hard to come by, and competition was fierce. Frustrated at his failure to get a job, Paresh's father had opted for self-employment. With the little money he had saved, he bought himself a rickshaw. Although city life was changing fast, there was still a demand for cycle rickshaws in those days. He managed to earn enough to put Paresh, his only child, in school.

Paresh proved to be an able pupil, clearing his examinations with high enough scores to go to University. He was the first from his family to boast of a university degree. Despite his academic achievements, a job remained out of his reach. He was too educated to pedal a cycle rickshaw. More importantly, earning a decent living as a rickshaw puller was no longer possible anyway. Motorcycles and four-wheelers had become the standard conveyance for most city folks.

As Paresh gathered from our conversation that I was living in America, he asked, 'Sir, how much do drivers earn in America?'

'I don't know.'

'Surely, you own a car. I hear people in America have more than one car; some have a fleet. Do you mind telling me how much you pay your driver?'

'I wish I could afford a driver. I don't have the luxury of having a driver at my beck and call.'

We had just stopped at a traffic light, waiting for it to change. Paresh looked at me with disbelief. But he tried to hide his true feelings with a polite grunt and said, 'I assumed you had a driver, as I gather, you had settled abroad for years. I hope you do not mind my curiosity.'

'Don't worry. Your question does not upset me, let alone offend me. But tell me, why do you ask?'

'I am sure you have guessed it, sir.'

'Not really.'

'I don't want you to get the wrong idea, Sir. Anupam-sir pays me quite handsomely, more than most drivers I know. He is also very generous in many other ways. But I hear there are opportunities for drivers abroad.'

'Do not worry; I won't let Anupam-sir know about this conversation. In fact, I won't tell anyone.'

It seemed he believed me and opened up, 'I am told drivers over there earn a lot more than what we make here. You must have friends and contacts. Perhaps, you fix a job for me in America.'

His naive question showed he had no idea of the complexities surrounding immigration and visa requirements for employment in America. I knew a simple yes or no would not go down well. Any quick attempt to explain would be fraught with danger, as he would misinterpret it as an unwillingness to help.

Conveniently, we had reached Anupam's home. The journey's end gave me an excuse to shelve the conversation. 'You see, the process is complicated and will take some time to explain. We will have to leave it for another ride.'

As I left the car, I reassured him, 'Remember, I won't forget to have a chat again.'

***

In Anupam's house, I was half expecting to see his wife, Archana. I had heard from Anupam about Archana's heavy involvement in charity work, which brought with it frequent social engagements. She had such a packed schedule that she could not join us on the ride to the reunion venue. She was going to join us later in the evening.

Nonetheless, Archana did manage to steal a few minutes from her crowded diary to speak to me briefly over the phone. 'I need to talk about Anupam with you,' she said.

'What is it about; is it about his health?'

'The matter is rather delicate to discuss on the phone. I fear Anupam is undergoing a midlife crisis.' Archana sounded weary. 'Anyway, you will be with us for a few days. We must find some time to talk. It will have to be done in private and face-to-face. Don't mention my concerns to him. Wait until we have a chance to talk first.'

By then, Anupam had arrived home. Archana promptly ended the call, saying, 'We will talk soon.'

I was left guessing about this new worry of Archana.

***

Back in the car, Anupam and I were approaching our destination, a popular resort in a hill station, a favourite venue for our college reunions. Anupam's phone rang, and he spoke briefly, ending the call with, 'I really can't talk now. Can I call you later?'. He turned to me, 'We have arrived at least a couple of hours before time. I just remembered I had a meeting that had been postponed. I would have to attend to this unfinished business today. I am hoping to get over this in the spare time in hand.'

'Oh, yes. It is just as well – I wanted to visit the Tibetan sanctuary nearby. I know you have little interest in it. So, I didn't mind doing it on my own while you have your meeting. This will suit both of us fine.'

'That sounds perfect. Paresh will drop me off at the hotel and drive you back to the sanctuary. See you later.'

Anupam got out of the car, and Paresh drove on. On the way to the sanctuary, Archana messaged me: 'Hi, Can you keep an eye on Anupam's movements at the holiday resort? I can't explain my reasons until I meet you. Nor can I talk about it now.'

'Of course, I will, if you want. But what should I look out for?' I texted back.

'I believe he is on a secret rendezvous with a lady. Follow him discreetly, but keep your eyes and ears open. Get me anything you can manage to find about her.'

I was not prepared for such a bombshell. I also felt Archana overestimated my detective skills or my ability to spy, to be more precise. *Perhaps, I could get a lead from Paresh.* I was certain Paresh would know the secret behind Anupam's announcement of this last-minute meeting.

'Paresh, Anupam-sir tells me you have been his most trustworthy driver, and he does not go anywhere without you.' I introduced my question discretely.

'Sir, I am very content with this job. My enquiry about working abroad was no more than simple curiosity. I have no plan to leave Sir's employment soon. He must not get any hint of our conversation lest he misinterprets it.'

'Of course, I understand your position. The spirit of ambition and aspiration suits a bright young man like you.'

I paused momentarily before putting my question in a controlled voice. 'You have my promise, Paresh. Can I ask you for a favour in return?'

He looked at me, surprised.

'Paresh, we are all curious in our own ways. I am wondering about this sudden meeting that Anupam-sir announced.'

'I am not sure, sir.'

'You have been close to Anupam-sir for so long. You

may not be sure, but you can make a guess. You have my guarantee; anything you tell me will stay with me. Not a soul will find out.'

'I have no idea, sir.'

'Do you have any inkling who Anupam-sir is meeting with right now as we speak?' I asked.

A sheepish Paresh replied, 'Sir, I know my position and my limits. I dare not stray beyond the boundary of my remit. My job is to drive Sir around, not delve into his private world'.

Hmm, I reflected. *Everyone is entitled to a quota of white lies, which come in handy in the unwritten civic code of confidentiality!*

The Song of the Cemetery

Over the years, Tonmoy must have visited the deserted ruins of Potagarh many times. Literally meaning 'buried fort' and situated not far from his home, it was indeed a forgotten site. He could not recall many visitors when he would visit Potagarh. He had no idea when it was built and how it came to be a derelict site. Although by name a fort, it was hard to tell whether it was a royal retreat or a garrison. That said, Tonmoy had an unexplainable connection with Potagarh.

Potagarh consisted of a cluster of structures in varying stages of dilapidation on the banks of River Subarnarekha ('streak of gold' in the local language). Its grand arched gateway was crumbling, but its massive rampart and prominent bastions attested to its gravitas in bygone days. Two impressive tunnels connected the fort via a secret passage to the riverbank.

Returning to Potagarh after years, Tonmoy was filled with a sense of adventure and anticipation. Armed with new knowledge, the prospect of rediscovering his old haunt filled him with the excitement of an explorer on a journey of discovery.

His return to Potagarh was met with pleasant surprises. The once dirt track leading to the ruins had turned into a concrete road, with signposts guiding the way. The sight of a small office with a sign reading '*Information*

Centre' and a crowd of locals and foreigners milling about filled him with joy and hope for the future of Potagarh. He gathered UNESCO money had transformed the long-neglected Potagarh into a historic attraction for visitors from far and wide.

Tonmoy remembered wandering around the complex, often all alone. His mind would usually roll back in time into the lives of people it housed perhaps hundreds of years ago. The secret tunnels connecting the core building to the riverbank hinted at the exalted status of people living there, who needed to escape from danger via the river. A sense of sadness would come over him as he thought of the departed hubbub of activity on Potagarh's grounds, leaving its corridors and gardens lifeless, even for birds or animals. As if to beat the melancholy, his mind would drift again as his imagination took a free run at conjuring images of the fort's former grandeur.

***

Tonmoy moved out of his native Odisha, first to Delhi and then to England, where he settled for a quarter of a century. But, his fascination with Potagarh never waned, and his curiosity about life in the forgotten fort never left him.

By a stroke of luck, Judith, a work colleague, mentioned her connection to India one day. As they talked, Tonmoy shared his past and life in his hometown in eastern India. Its name was not worth a mention; it was too insignificant to be known inside India, let alone abroad. The nearest city, well-known in England, was Calcutta. As he mentioned it, Judith's ears perked up. Her great-grandfather had lived in India for many years, somewhere not far from Calcutta.

On his next visit to Judith's house, the conversation eventually turned to their common interest: India. In the gathering, alongwith Judith were her sister Stella, Stella's husband, and an uncle, all visiting Judith for a family celebration. Judith and her family shared some fond memories from her great-grandfather's time in India, which were passed on to her by her parents.

'You know, Tony (Judith had anglicised his name, as did many of his colleagues, for obvious reasons), it's difficult for us to imagine the lives of Englishmen and women who called India their second home. For many, it was truly their home as they lived the better part of their lives in India, and some, of course, died there.'

Tonmoy nodded, 'It is not easy, especially at first, to live in a faraway land among people with strange customs and unfamiliar habits. But all said and done, their lives in India certainly did not lack excitement, as the place was full of action.'

'Yes, we have heard many tales of romance, betrayal and intrigue. One is a touching but tragic love story my grandfather told us,' Judith said.

Tonmoy's jaw dropped when he first saw the treasure Judith showed him that evening – a hundred-year-old love poem. It came from an Englishman, Alfred Stanbrook, written by his fiancée during their courtship. As the story went, Alfred fell in love with a young local widow. They were about to marry, but their affair ended tragically with her premature death. Alfred spent the rest of his life in India single. He did not have any family, and upon his death, the poem came into the possession of Judith's great-grandfather, his closest friend in India. Ever since, it had been a family heirloom.

'Their love was the stuff of novels and films, a saga sublime and tragic at once. The poem is believed to be the epitome of love, expressed in the most exquisite words.

But it is written in an Indian language no one can read. The original paper on which it was written is gone. This is a copy,' Judith explained before handing the poem to Tonmoy.

He stared at it, his eyes popping out in disbelief. ‹What was the name of the place in India where your great-grandfather worked?' he asked.

'We don't know. Can you read the poem, Tony?' Judith asked.

Tonmoy said, 'I never imagined I would find a poem, written in my mother tongue, from more than a century ago, in a land thousands of miles away.'

He read it silently, his heart racing with excitement and disbelief. All eyes were glued, expectantly, to his face. He was not sure he grasped the poem fully. He read it again, mulling over how to paraphrase it, his mind filled with wonder, curiosity, and a tinge of profound sadness for the tragic love story it narrated.

'It is high poetry, making it hard to translate,' he uttered finally. A woman in love has poured her heart out, but there is a touch of ambivalence in her feelings for her beloved. It seems she feels unworthy of the adoration of her beloved. But it's clear why it was so precious to Alfred. It's a masterpiece of poetry, a treasure in its own right.'

The love story of Alfred Stanbrook fuelled Tonmoy's curiosity about the history of the East India Company and the British Raj. He took note of as many details as he could from Judith of her great-grandfather and Alfred. After many hours of research in the Indian section of the British Library, he gathered Alfred worked somewhere close to his hometown, and his resting place was by River *Subarnarekha*, an area he knew well. In the process, Tonmoy learned a lot about Potagarh's history. His findings pointed to a tantalising possibility: Alfred's grave might be somewhere around the fort complex of Potagarh. The story of Alfred and his beloved, written in Tonmoy's mother tongue, deepened his connection to the historical site and its love story.

***

The new look of Potagarh filled Tonmoy with immense satisfaction. At long last, it had received its due recognition as a historical monument. His curiosity about the newly erected official plaques nudged him to study them. But, all that reading would have to wait until he first checked the tombstones in the cemetery, which lay at the farthest end of the complex. He remembered the cemetery from his previous visits: it had been in ruins, with only a handful of tombstones left standing.

"Do you need a guide, sir?" The voice came from behind as he hurried towards the cemetery. Lost in his own world, he continued after a cursory, 'No, thank you.'

In the past, he had not found the tombstones worth a second glance. However, during this visit, the cemetery was his central attraction. Previously, the European-sounding names did not mean much to him; it did not matter whether they were British, French, or Dutch. Now, they represented people of flesh and blood, like Alfred Stanbrook, not mere faceless foreigners. Alfred's love story had given Tonmoy's imagination a free ride.

Tonmoy was not sure how much of the cemetery still stood for him to explore. He was relieved to find the cemetery changed little. After wading through its labyrinthine passage, he reached the tombstones. Parts of the stones had fallen off, obliterating the names. The remaining letters on most had faded, obscuring the details of the epitaphs.

Moving briskly, he scanned the names until he spotted one he recognised: *Alfred Stanbrook*. Although many of the letters had disappeared, he was in no doubt. The name *Alfred Stanbrook* shone across the stones; thanks to the brain's magical power to recreate the missing letters. Only two digits were visible—1 and 8—the other numbers and letters were worn away. The plaque was too damaged to decipher the missing digits.

Tonmoy stood staring at the grave, imagining the life Englishman Alfred Stanbrook spent in this remote land more than a hundred years ago. He didn't know how long he had been standing there when his reverie was broken by the same voice he had heard as he made his way to the cemetery.

He turned around to see a middle-aged lady with a beaming smile, asking again, "Do you need a guide, sir?" She was of average height, dressed in a blue skirt with a flowery pattern, which suited her complexion. Her face was oblong, set against her bobbed hair, which bounced gently as she spoke.

'I never thought I would see guides in Potagarh. I have been visiting this place for ages, and usually, I am the only visitor. Anyway, I am so glad you are here.' Tonmoy continued, "But perhaps, for a change, I shall be your guide today'.

She looked quizzically at him.

'I bet you don't know much about this tombstone,' Tonmoy said, turning his head towards the remains of Alfred's epitaph. He recounted his long association with Potagarh and the extensive research into its history he had undertaken in England.

'You know, I could write a doctoral thesis on Potagarh. But that would pale in comparison with what I have discovered about Alfred Stanbrook's life.' Pointing at the tombstone, he said, 'This is his final resting ground'.

With great excitement, he began to relate the love story of Englishman Alfred Stanbrook. 'He lived his short life in India, working for the East India Company. He fell in love with a young local woman whose life was a litany of woes. She had been given in marriage as a child bride, and upon attaining puberty, she was sent off for matrimonial union with her husband at the tender age of thirteen.

'Sadly, her conjugal bliss did not last long; it was shattered in less than a year's time by her husband's tragic death. She returned to her parents for a condemned and miserable existence. Those days, a widow's remarriage was unheard of, and she knew any prospect of marriage was bleak. By a twist of fate, Lady Fortune smiled upon her when Alfred entered her life. Alfred was enamoured by her beauty and charm, and soon a relationship blossomed.'

The guide listened to Tonmoy in rapt attention.

'Alfred was sincere in pursuing her, but to his surprise, he found her response lukewarm. Alfred was an eligible bachelor, and the idea of an Englishman marrying a native woman, a widow, was not received favourably in Alfred's social circle. But, the bigger hurdle, apparently, was her opposition. She believed that she was a jinxed soul and would bring misfortune to anyone she loved. So, she resisted his advances for a pretty long time.'

'How did Alfred's love story end?' She asked.

'Yes! Alfred was not one to give up easily. He pursued his lady love doggedly, and it took him years to shake her off her superstitious ideas. His love had already won her heart; finally, his patience and perseverance changed her mind, too. She was eventually convinced that their love deserved a chance to live on, and they were set to marry. But their affair was truly jinxed, as she died suddenly of a mysterious illness when she was barely in her twenties. Her death dealt a devastating blow to Alfred, who never married and spent the rest of his life as a single man. He died in India and was buried here in Potagarh.'

The guide watched Tonmoy's face closely while he was engrossed in telling Alfred's story, totally unaware of her reactions to his monologue. 'Are you, by any chance, from Austin Hubback High School?' she asked suddenly.

Tonmoy's mind had floated back in time by more than a century to the world of Alfred Stanbrook. The mention of his school jolted his mind back to his school days. His eyes were drawn to the name badge on the guide's dress; it read *Alice*. His high school and the name Alice, put together, switched on the lights of his dim vault of memory.

'And you finished high school in 1985?' she continued.

'So, it's you, Alice!' he exclaimed. 'Oh, Alice, you recognised me before I could place you.'

His face changed colour in embarrassment; it took him so long to recognise her. But thirty-odd years is long by any stretch, and over this time, her looks had changed. As he imagined the young Alice, memories of their school days flooded his mind. He was lost again, now in a world of his own past.

***

For four years, teenagers Alice and Tonmoy were classmates in school. In those days, contact between boys and girls was restricted; physical intimacy was limited to holding hands. However, their friendship took a romantic turn; by their final year, their mutual attraction had reached its peak. He remembered spending hours daydreaming of their romance blossoming into a blissful life together. But he found Alice holding herself back, never fully reciprocating his advances.

Tonmoy was not blind to Alice's predicament; he knew what was bugging her. Alice was Christian and from the tribal class, an *adivasi*[16]. Her class was way below Tonmoy's upper-class Hindu status. Their religious divide was deep, and their social standings were a world apart. His father was the local collector, while Alice came from a humble background.

Tonmoy tried to reassure Alice that their pure love would overcome their social differences. But Alice could not see herself ever fitting into his world. His frustrations grew as he found his most sincere love was not enough to dispel her doubts over their future.

After finishing school, they parted ways. Tonmoy went off to the college in the city. His father got posted out and eventually retired in their ancestral town. He kept in touch with Alice through letters for months, trying to woo her in the hope of eventually changing her mind. However, it came to nothing as Alice's ever-growing hesitation kept souring his feelings for her. A logical Alice kept reminding Tonmoy that he was a dreamer.

With the passage of years, they lost all contact, and this chapter of his life became a distant memory. The demands of his job and career gradually took over his life. He never imagined in his wildest dreams of seeing Alice again.

****

After so many years, they had met again. It got them

---

16 Adivasi: Literally means 'indigenous people' and refers to the tribal population of the Indian subcontinent. It is a collective term for the aboriginal or the original inhabitants of the land. Many *adivasis* in Odisha converted to Christianity under the influence of missionaries.

to share their life stories. Tonmoy had moved on and had settled in England for decades, where his profession took centre stage in his life. Alice, too, had broken grounds; she became the first woman in their family to attend University, and she chose the life of a working woman.

As Tonmoy continued with the love story of Alfred Stanbrook, he remembered his last rendezvous with Alice. It was a rare opportunity they had managed to steal that allowed them to talk at some length. Beforehand, they could meet in privacy for barely a few minutes at a time. He had been living in hope all along, convinced that his love for Alice would ultimately prevail. They discussed all sorts of challenges in store in their life together and considered the necessary compromises to turn their dream of marriage into a reality. Tonmoy understood her apprehensions but found her approach to solving the problems half-hearted and unduly pessimistic about their future.

He was well aware of his parents' opposition to their marriage. However, he was confident that he would eventually persuade them to accept her. He just needed more time to work on their objections. However, his mighty persuasiveness, which he knew would work on his parents, proved tame against stubborn Alice.

All his pleadings fell flat at her resolve. Nothing could shift her from the view that their love had no future. Her unwavering position was that the best they could do was to give it a decent burial. Tonmoy felt the last vestiges of hope slip away. Between the two of them, perhaps Alice was a better judge of the future of their affair. He finally accepted that their love was doomed.

A bleak reality was dawning over his dream world.

He could clearly visualise Alice's face lit in the bright moonlight of that evening. He could hear the lapping sea waves and feel the gentle breeze. He vividly remembered drawing closer to Alice. When he cupped her face in his palms, his entire body felt electrified. As their lips met, he felt Alice's body quiver. Soon, their bodies were locked in a deep embrace and the world outside simply evaporated. The rest of that evening was a blur. That was their last meeting.

****

'Wow, what a discovery, Tonmoy!' Alice said as Tonmoy came to the end of Alfred's doomed love story.

Tonmoy's trance was broken. Dragged back to the present, he said, 'Ah, you haven't yet heard the exquisite poem from his beloved, which Alfred treasured all his life'.

While Alice looked at him in surprise, he pulled out a piece of paper from his pocket. Unfolding it with his shaking hands, he was about to hand it to Alice. Instead, he read it aloud.

My Heart Murmured[17]
My heart murmured,
but did it utter anything?
That's how hearts speak.

And my heart heard something;
but how? It was almost inaudible!
Such are the ways of the heart.

My heart getting restless in anticipation;
it's beyond me to contain it.
I fear my yearnings might force open my eyes,
only to bring disgrace.

Better to let the dream fairy sleep,
undisturbed, on my cosy eyelids.
Such are the ways of the heart.
I adorn myself with fake glitter and sparkle,

---

17 This poem is embroidered on Kaifi Azmi's lyrics for the song, 'Kuchh dil ne kaha' from the Hindustani film *Anupama* (1966).

just to console my heart.
Everyone taken in by the facade of spring in my life,
despite the void within.

Yet, nobody bothers to check
whether the crying buds' tears
are from joy or sorrow.
Such are the ways of the heart.

My heart murmured something,
I can barely decode.
Such are the ways of the heart.......

Alice listened intently, spellbound. *Somebody, somewhere, a long time ago, could read my mind*, she thought.

Her thoughts were interrupted by Tonmoy's question, 'Did you say something?'

'Could you hear it?' Alice asked.

'Not sure what I heard. What do you make of the poem?'

'That is how I felt that evening on the seashore,' Alice whispered.

Tonmoy looked at Alice as she stood against the ravages of Potagarh in the distance. An ethereal glow from the setting sun permeated the entire place. As her words resonated in the recesses of his mind, her face, framed by the ruins in the background, turned radiant. He turned his gaze to Alfred's tombstone as if looking for the remnants of their own teenage love buried somewhere in its rubble. The mystique of the ruins, which had puzzled him all along, was beginning to unravel.

Dreams Men Live For

The park was deserted. The children's play area had been quiet for months. The hubbub of activity in the playground was now only a distant memory. The lockdown mandated by emergency COVID-19 laws to protect the public from the ravages of Coronavirus was becoming increasingly oppressive. The play area felt the pinch, too, as it suffered from a complete absence of children. They were safely kept at bay by their responsible parents, dutifully complying with the law of the land. The sign on the play area's gate read: *Following Government advice on the current COVID-19 pandemic, playground Closed for the foreseeable future.*

The swing stood still, in an expectant mood, as if it was waiting for a signal from somewhere to start moving again. The slide was a forlorn sight. It seemed to be scanning the surroundings for children who might slip underneath their parents' watchful eyes to innocently defy the ban and come running to climb its ladder. The static see-saw stood poised to burst forth into activity any time. With its knotted ropes making a square pattern, the climbing frame stood silently, longing for tiny hands and feet to pull on them.

John was strolling in the park with all his possessions in a backpack. A young man now, barely into his late teens, he had been homeless for about a year. The chaos at home brought about by his parents' disorganised life had troubled him for years, and the situation had lately become unbearable. As soon as he turned eighteen, he left home for an itinerant lifestyle in the city.

Living on the streets was not entirely fun, but he had taken it in his stride and had settled into a routine. The anonymity of city life presented him with the solitude he desperately sought. There was no dearth of space for sleeping at night, thanks to the numerous nooks and crannies the massive office buildings of the city offered. Food was plentiful and free. He could even manage to earn a decent sum towards his pocket money from busking. As long as he kept his nose clean, the police hardly bothered him.

This harmonious equilibrium was disrupted by COVID-19, which triggered the Lockdown Law, with its draconian infringements of civil liberty, unprecedented in peaceful times: leaving home was forbidden, except for shopping for food, picking up medicine, doing essential work, or emergencies. Breach of this embargo was an offence punishable with instant fines, and thousands of cops were deployed to enforce the law.

But the new law threw the government into a quandary. Homeless people could not be 'locked down' simply because they had no home to lock them in. That reality brought in a new government initiative to provide temporary housing for all the city's rough sleepers.

The change was a shattering blow to John's peaceful existence. He did not fancy the accommodation the authorities had arranged for him. The idea of compulsory confinement suffocated his free spirit. Moreover, the last thing he wanted was the company of other homeless people. All their talk of difficult home circumstances and troubled childhoods stirred up painful memories of his own past he was trying to forget. So, he was on the run.

He walked out of the city centre as far as his legs could carry him. There are too many cops in the city, he thought; he had to get away from the glare of the patrolling police. All he wanted was a quiet place to spend the night.

When he came upon it, the children's play area looked like a perfect hideout. He put his backpack down and sat on the bench. He could not remember when he last entered a playground. When he was a child, playgrounds were rather basic in design and equipment. The chaos of his childhood left his parents little time to accompany him to play in a park like this.

The tranquil air and gentle breeze made the atmosphere soporific. Exhausted by the long walk, he soon drifted off to sleep.

The presence of a boy – *though older than most who used to play here* – stirred the swing, the see-saw, and the slide into action as if awakened from hibernation.

As night fell, the playground came alive, as if by the touch of a magic wand. The slide winked at the swing, which, in turn, let out a faint whistle at the see-saw. They all had to contain their excitement and keep calm; no one wanted to disturb their guest's sleep. Soon, though, they all swung into action to entertain this oversized guest. The playground transformed into a fairyland.

John dreamt he was a little boy in a wheelchair, positioned in the middle of a magical playground. The boy looked longingly at the array of equipment surrounding him. His floppy legs did not have enough strength to lift him to any of them. He shifted his glance from one structure to the next. This only made his longing to play on them grow. The hopelessness of his situation built up inside, and finally, he let out a plaintive cry.

To his amazement, the legs of the slide's ladder began

to move in his direction, dragging the whole slide behind it. He gaped as it stopped near his wheelchair. He felt himself dragged from his wheelchair onto the slide's ladder. It was as if his body were a lump of metal wrenched out of the chair by a powerful magnet and let down onto the rungs of the slide's ladder.

As his floppy legs touched the ladder's lowest rung, a rush of energy thrust them into motion. He effortlessly climbed up the ladder, forgetting that he ever had weak legs. As he reached the top, he saw all the other playground structures gazing at him, pleading with him to come to them.

He came down the slide and plopped on the ground. He was again unable to move his legs. Wide-eyed, he saw the swing fly out at him and pick him up in its seat. Soon, he was swinging in the air, enjoying the splash of cool breeze on his face. The pleasure of getting to a height from where he could catch a glimpse of the lights at the edge of the city was evident on his face.

As the swing finally came to a stop, his eyes caught the see-saw at the other end of the play area. It was stretching itself towards him. One end of the see-saw gently lowered itself close to the ground. It pushed itself between the ground and his legs. In a scooping movement, the see-saw raised him off the ground. Soon, he was going up and down in the air with the playground fairy sitting at the other end of the see-saw, giving him company and the thrust for the up-and-down movement.

The boy's eyes popped out in wonder. When he looked up, he saw the field surrounding the play section had changed into a colourful garden. It had winding paths lined with neatly trimmed holly hedges. Beyond the hedges were rows of trees creating a pattern of flowing lines as far back as the eyes could see. Their glistening red berries stood out against the shiny green leaves. Beyond the hedges were rows of trees lining the paths, crisscrossing the landscape. Flowers dotted the ground, their colours ranging from pastel shades of lilac, peach and yellow to vibrant red and ultramarine blue. Squirrels and rabbits frolicked in playful abandon. The chirping of sparrows and robins filled the air with mirth and merriment. Their chatter was complemented by the gentle gurgling of a brook flowing through the garden.

He did not have a word for what he was seeing. *Perhaps this is what paradise looks like!* With a newfound mobility and sense of freedom, the enchanting vista ushered waves of energy and excitement in the boy. Although he wanted to explore the garden forthwith, he was unsure how to start or where to go first.

The little boy was having the time of his life. He forgot that he had floppy legs and needed a wheelchair to get around. But his luck didn't last long.

A gentle thumping noise sounded from a distance, gradually getting louder. Soon, the thud on the ground got heavier, too. The boy saw the silhouette of a giant moving towards him. It was like an enormous blob on the horizon, growing steadily larger. The light faded, and the scene turned grey as if dark clouds had descended upon the park. The ogre, by now, occupied almost the entire field of his vision. As it drew nearer, he could see the ogre's scowling face, marching towards him with a mace in his hand.

The ogre made a growling noise shaking his entire body. He was shouting in a language which was beyond his comprehension. The menacing sight and frightful noise made his heart race. He wanted to flee – but his legs would not move.

A raucous voice announced: 'Didn't you see the notice on the gate of this play area? It says, *it is closed.'*

He stirred his legs and realised they could move. He'd been fast asleep. From the bench, lying on his back, John opened his eyes. His vision was blurred. He rubbed his eyes to focus on what was dangling close to his face.

It was no ogre's mace; it was the tip of a cop's baton.

The House with a Tree

When the lockdown was announced in the wake of the COVID-19 pandemic, it never crossed my mind that it would drag on for so long. At the outset, it was no more than a minor inconvenience, but everything began to change as days rolled into weeks and months.

I ran a successful consultancy firm, providing logistical advice to companies for their supply needs. My service was highly rated, and my opinion was sought after. But neither my experience nor my reputation could prop up my business. It soon buckled under the unprecedented calamity ushered by the pandemic and the ensuing lockdown. My speciality is projection of future supply, contingency and procurement needs. However, the research budgets of most companies dried up during the lockdown. All my expertise fell flat on its face from the pandemic's knock-out punch. My company's cash flow dwindled, and the financial strain showed. I had already run into mortgage arrears with the bank while my application for government aid had stalled in an administrative maze.

The lockdown allowed going out only for emergencies, procuring food and medicines, and a limited amount of exercise. The first few days felt like a compulsory holiday with a 22-hour curfew. It gradually turned into a virtual prison sentence, a solitary confinement with up to two hours of leave outdoors. The absence of routine and structure to the day was slowly but surely making its mark.

The boredom of lockdown soon turned into a burden, getting heavier over time with added anxieties and uncertainties. To kill the monotony, I varied my daily chores, devising a new routine for each day. But nothing seemed to work. I had to capitalise on the only saving grace of the lockdown: exercise outdoors. I extended my walking routine and explored new routes.

The routes gradually became more elaborate, covering new territories I had never ventured before. My standard track was in the open fields, stretching several miles. Now, I was walking beyond the fields into the next village. On the way were sporadic houses, standing singly or in clusters of three to four. On one such route, I noticed a FOR SALE sign from a distance outside a house. As I got closer, the house came into full view. What grabbed my attention first was the Magnolia tree in full bloom in its forecourt.

The captivating colour of its flowers stopped me in my tracks. They were a soothing shade of pink, far from flashy, as if the tree was caught in the desire to show off its splendour, reined in by its own coyness. I had seen many flowering trees before, but the ineffable charm of this Magnolia was arresting.

The sign board was rather plain, matching the ordinariness of the house. There was no realtor's name, just a telephone number. 'Perhaps it's a private sale by the owner to save on the commission,' I thought.

I immediately called the number. My guess was correct; the owner was selling the house without involving an agent. 'This is not an ordinary sale,' he said. 'I do not trust any realtor to handle this special job, so I decided to do it myself.'

After confirming my interest in the property, the owner asked about my interests and hobbies.

I was miffed; it was certainly an odd line of enquiry.

'What's the property on the market for?' I asked.

The figure he quoted surprised me, as it was substantially lower than I expected. 'There must be something wrong with the property,' I told myself. Lest I'd misheard, I asked him to repeat it to confirm the asking price.

The throwaway asking price fuelled my curiosity about the property. The magnificent Magnolia tree was staring at me. I could not help asking, 'Does the price include the premium for the magnificent Magnolia?'

'Yes, the price reflects the tree you are talking about, but not as you imagine. The asking price for the property is half of its market value. This steep discount of 50 per cent comes with a special condition that the buyer will preserve...'

I interrupted before he finished the sentence: 'Of course, the Magnolia tree is so pretty; it would be a crime to chop it down. In fact, the tree got me interested in this property in the first place.'

I anticipated a premium for the tree, which would have inflated the asking price. I could not work out how the tree would account for a 50% discount. I was mentally prepared with a strategy for bargaining on the premium the owner would demand for the tree. But the seller's unexpected and massive discount on the asking price, not to mention the bonus of this charming Magnolia, threw me in a quandary.

While I pondered over this incredibly mysterious bargain, the owner piped up, 'No, it's more demanding than that.....,' and he paused for my response.

I was trying to understand what the demand might be.

'You must preserve the tree and its attached...'

'Of course, I will preserve the tree exactly as it is.' I added impatiently.

'That's good, but you must also preserve the attached memories!'

'That's a strange condition. How does one preserve memories attached to a tree? You carry your memories with you, don't you?'

'Yes, I know, but the tree was planted by my father, who has since died. He could not take the memories with him when he died, and he entrusted them to me for their safekeeping.'

He continued, 'If my father could not take them, could they ever be safe with me? They are best vested in the tree, and the new owner must take on the responsibility of preserving them.'

'But how would you know if the new owner is honouring the commitment?'

There was a brief silence.

'How can I prove that I will fulfil this condition?' I asked.

'I know it is tricky, but it would be up to the new owner to find a way. That is what the substantial discount is for.'

It threw me totally off balance. I was intrigued by this unusual house and its owner's novel condition for the sale. I scratched my head. *Was this a joke? Or a trap? Or a test of my intelligence?* I had plenty of tasks demanding my urgent attention. There were quite a few items in my to-do list for immediate action. But this new challenge absorbed me totally over everything else in my mind.

'I must leave now. Can we continue this discussion tomorrow?' the owner said, abruptly ending the call, and leaving me with more questions than answers.

***

That night, I dreamt I was in a foreign land. I could

not make out which country it was. I had been walking for hours, exhausted and ready to hit the bed. But I did not have any accommodation.

I was desperate for information on how to get a room for the night, but there was nobody to whom I could turn for help. I encountered countless people on my path. I kept my ears glued to their conversations, hoping to catch something I could understand. But I had no luck; I could not catch a single word of theirs that made sense.

All the signs were in a foreign script, perhaps Chinese, Japanese or Korean. I could not make out which one, as they all looked alike to me. The evening had fallen, and it had started to get dark.

I approached several people with questions about overnight accommodations. I used all the possible words: hotel, motel, guest house, bed-sit, bed and breakfast, room for the night. I hoped someone could give me a lead, but I had no such luck. Obviously, they did not understand me.

Then I spotted a man in a suit and a hat. My hopes were raised, and I ran towards him. Even if he spoke in broken English, at least I could get some idea, some clue to work on. As I got closer, I heard him talking with a man beside him. I pinned my ears to their conversation.

As I approached them, their chatting grew louder and their words clearer. As I prepared myself to ask, 'Do you speak English?', I realised the question was redundant. They were engrossed in conversation that was music to my ears. It was in flawless English with perfect diction! As I reached them, I heard the man saying clearly to his companion, 'Once you figure this out, everything will fall into place.'

***

My dream was interrupted by the ringing alarm, waking me up for my walk.

The house with the tree was fresh on my mind. I wanted to take a good look at it again, so I started on the route I had taken the previous day. Everything had a surreal feel. As I reached the spot of the bungalow with the tree, I was shocked. There was no house and no tree either! I walked further and looked around, checking, all in vain. Was I missing something obvious?

The huge discount on the asking price for the house was topped only by the mind-boggling condition attached to it. *'This stuff about keeping his father's memories of the Magnolia tree is bewildering. The bargain of the century is really no bargain as it comes with an impossible demand. Now, I can't even find the house.'* My head was beginning to spin.

Had I taken a wrong turn on my walk? Maybe, in my mental disarray, I had forgotten the route I took yesterday. It was, after all, a new route for me. Open fields, like the sea, lack landmarks; it can disorient you. 'Yes, I am losing my mental bearings,' I concluded.

'Preserve the attached memories...' The phrase lingered, repeating itself in my mind. The owner wanted his father's memories to be kept and protected.

My father had been dead for decades. It was so long since he'd passed on that he hardly came into my thoughts. I'd even stopped dreaming of him. Then, last night came the intriguing dream. I was puzzled. 'The lockdown, surely, has taken its toll on me,' I said to myself, 'but it is now driving me crazy.'

Everything felt fuzzy; I could not be certain where reality ended and the dream began.

Then, it occurred to me that something had slipped out of my mind for the first time: yesterday was the anniversary of my father's death.

Something Understood

Every dog owner knows the benefits of having a dog as a pet. Health benefits come to mind first. Walking a dog almost religiously, come rain or shine, or snow, for that matter, imposes a minimum dose of physical activity, a tonic against the toxicity of a sedentary life. A dog enlivens a home's emotional atmosphere, bringing the whole family together. For me, our family dog provided an entirely unforeseen positive effect on my social life.

Until we got our first dog, a Border Collie, I was almost a stranger in the small English village that had been our home for years. Of course, I could not go about unnoticed as we were the only family of colour in an almost exclusively white village. I accepted it, though not wholeheartedly, putting it down to the English reserve, which makes it hard to warm up to someone who looks different.

Our dog had a pitch-black coat against which the shining white stripe on his neck and face stood out. His eyes had a twinkle; they were so expressive that he could talk with them. Although he had a playful nature, he was calm by temperament. We named him Raja (pronounced as Rājā) – an Indian name meaning 'king'. It could not have been more apt as the entire household danced to his tune. Our bond with Raja was as deep as that with our children. Strangely, over time, Raja became closer to us than our children. Unlike the children who left home to go to university, Raja stayed. Raja was our child who never grew up!

As I began to walk Raja, the change in the villagers' response towards me was noticeable. I now struck up conversations with many during my walks whom I had seen before but had never interacted with. Raja must take some credit for this; he was remarkably well-behaved on the road. He was the first dog in the village that went everywhere without a leash. I doubt many knew my name, but most of these acquaintances probably got to know me only by our dog's name: 'You know the man with the dog with an Indian name – Raja.'

Most people I came across during such walks were friendly; at the least, they would reciprocate my greeting, and some would engage in a brief conversation. But there was one exception – a lady I saw often would not acknowledge my presence. In the beginning, I was unsure if she heard my greetings. So, I thought, I must give her the benefit of the doubt.

The next time our paths crossed, I made it a point to slow down when approaching her. I almost stopped briefly before greeting her, 'Good morning,' articulating the words distinctly. But again, there was no response whatsoever.

Did she hear me? I wondered.

However, there was no mistake in my mind as to whether she heard me or not. She certainly saw me uttering the words even if she did not hear them. I made allowances for the possibility that she was hard of hearing, but she could not be blind also. She could not avoid reading my lips.

The scene repeated itself again and again. I must admit, however hard I tried to rationalise her behaviour, I felt hurt by her indifference. I became convinced she was deliberately avoiding me and had resolved not to talk to me.

Days rolled into weeks and then into months. Her response was the same in every encounter, no different from the first.

So, what else could it be? It must be a subtle form of racism. She is white, and I am brown, and that is that.

I wish I could have let it rest at that. But I was smarting from my pricked pride. It lingered like an irritation from a speck of dust stuck in my eye, which I just couldn't shake off.

One day, I was in a contemplative mood when our paths crossed again, and the old experience was repeated. It suddenly occurred to me: Could she be mute? This would be a perfectly logical explanation for her behaviour. This mere possibility eased my sense of hurt and brought in a tinge of guilt for labelling her attitude racist.

But the next time I saw her from a distance, I heard her talking with someone. That incident dispelled my theory of mutism and seemed to confirm my worst fear: racism had to be the sole explanation for her haughtiness.

With time, my resentment gradually receded. But the hurt of being ignored did not wholly leave me.

I still saw her occasionally, but I stopped greeting her and changed my direction to avoid crossing her path.

Soon, the whole saga became a footnote in this chapter of my life.

***

A few months later, I was in a pensive mood. Raja had been ill for a few weeks, and the vet had diagnosed cancer. There was no viable treatment, and the prognosis was grim. He was not his usual lively self and, indeed, not keen on his usual walks anymore.

On the footpath, I noticed I was about to cross past the woman who never greeted me. I did not have the energy to change direction to avoid her that day. Somewhat uncharacteristically, she stopped as we were about to pass. Looking at Raja, she asked, 'Is he not well?'

I was taken by surprise. The question was totally unexpected from someone who hadn't even acknowledged my presence so far. I was pretty unprepared to make a suitable response to someone who, until today, had found it below her dignity to return my greetings.

Before I could think of something appropriate, I blurted, 'How did you know?'

'I guessed something must not be quite right with him. He is usually well ahead of you as if taking you for a walk. But he seems sluggish, and his eyes look sad.'

'Yes, you have got it right,' I said, debating in my mind how much detail I should give her.

'I can read it on your face,' she replied.

'He has got cancer, and it has spread already. And, he does not have long to live…' My voice faltered, and I could not continue. I was consumed by the prospect of Raja's imminent death.

She put her hand on my forearm and looked at my distraught face. I tried to avert my gaze out of sheer embarrassment. Her hand felt like the comforting caress of an angel to my bruised soul.

She looked at me silently for what seemed like an eternity. Before I gently moved my arm away, from the corner of my eyes, I caught her look, which clearly stated, 'I know how it feels'.

I regained my composure, and we chatted for a few more minutes about Raja's condition, diagnosis, and treatment – or lack thereof.

Just before she turned away to get back on her path, she said, 'Perhaps this is not the time to talk about me, but I assure you, this too will pass. About a year ago, my dog was ill, too, and the world around me simply ceased to exist. I was in a haze for months, oblivious to nearly everything and everybody except my dog, especially after he passed. But I pulled through, and so will you.'

As I slowly resumed my walk, I remembered how much I'd resented her until today. How naive I was to rely on language as the bedrock of communication and read her aloofness as an act of racism. My presumption had turned me blind to whatever she might be trying to say all along!

Grief can be all-consuming for the mind and dull all links with the outer world to near paralysis. I wondered how many people would misunderstand my absorption in my private world as indifference or, even worse, a sign of snobbery.

On my way home, the thought of losing Raja was still heavy on my mind, but I was feeling somewhat lighter. I did not know what did the trick: Solving the old puzzle of her haughty silence or having the burden of my pain eased by her soothing touch? Maybe there was something more to it.

Words are clever; they can say a lot. Sometimes, the eyes can speak better. Conveying the utterly unspeakable demands an altogether different touch: something shared between two souls, something understood.

The Big Picture

It started as a routine walk in the fields. The open stretches of land had become my silent companion in this morning ritual. On our very first encounter, the fields cast a spell on me. Although familiarity had taken some shine off their magic over the years, the fields never ceased to have their hold on me.

In summer, they radiate the yellow glow of rapeseed; in autumn, the colour changes to a golden red. Between seasons, when the land is lying fallow, the grounds come alive with captivating patterns of furrows carved out of the farmer's tractor. Their rugged contours follow no set rules of symmetry but are far from irregular. Although a dull brown in colour, their pleasing proportions are a joy to behold. The ground it seems is finally rewarded for its patience, lying long in wait for an opportunity to showcase its buried beauty.

But today, the fields looked dreary, as if they reflected my sombre mood. Until yesterday, I was in regular employment with an unbroken record of almost three decades. Secure in my steady job, I used to get ready for work after my morning walk. I operated on nearly an auto-pilot mode for the rest of the day. This routine lent a structure to my days, and time flew.

Today marked the beginning of a new chapter of my life. I didn't know what my day would bring after I finished my morning walk. Now, I had to plan my days with all my resources to find a new job.

As a manager in the bookstore chain, Cornerstones, I had a settled life. Cornerstones, one of the biggest players in the industry, projected prestige. I had worked methodically to move up the career ladder to a comfortable position. Though it was not without struggle, I had managed to stave off a single day of unemployment.

Most of my working life was in retail, with little experience outside. For several years, retail businesses have been reeling from the onslaught of customers' online shopping habits. This had accelerated during the pandemic. To kill the monotony of the lockdown, more and more people had picked up reading, and the sale of books was booming. But bookshops were shutting down at an alarming pace.

Like many companies, Cornerstones' sales had been badly hit by online book suppliers, and it had been grappling with dwindling profits. It added an online wing to its business to boost its revenues, but this was not enough to offset the high overheads from running high-street stores. As the workforce was shrinking and jobs were being axed steadily, my position as a middle manager was an easy target.

About two months ago, I received the news of my redundancy, which I had been dreading for a long time. It jolted me out of my sedate existence. The generous financial package, meant to soften the blow of unemployment, was little comfort. Apprehensions about my uncertain future made me despair over my long-term job prospects.

I had applied for several jobs, but many of them did not bother to reply. I guess the competition for the few posts I was chasing was too stiff. I even pursued junior jobs, but again, I had no luck, perhaps because I was considered overqualified. I was in my fifties, and the chance of finding a job in the current climate was slim. The prospect of life without a job was daunting. My future looked bleak.

I cast my mind back to my twenties; to my dreamy eyes of youth, nothing seemed out of reach. I remembered my passion for dramatics, which was at its height in my college days. There was a month-long spell in the middle of the academic year earmarked for the interclass dramatics competition. It was marked by a frenzy of activities. Brainstorming sessions on the script, stage management and special effects would be followed by field trips for collecting outdoor sound effects and rehearsals. Excitement would build to its peak on the Annual Day, culminating in the stage performance. Since finishing college, other priorities in life overshadowed all such passions. Demands of my job extracted the last ounce of my energy, leaving little for other pursuits. It sent all my dreams into hibernation. I put my life on hold, waiting for the fantasised golden period when I could be myself again.

Looking back at my life, I wondered if I had achieved much. My regrets would not have been so deep if I had, so far, lived a fulfilled life. I realised I had invested my entire being in my job. I had missed the fun of living for the sake of a livelihood. Now, that, too, is gone. I was at a crossroads; my life seemed empty of meaning or direction.

In my absent-mindedness, I left home on my walk without my phone. Listening to music is one of my favourite pastimes during my walks. It is such an enchanting experience, hard to beat and impossible to describe. Under the open sky, rhythms and melodies sound heavenly, as if Gods of music have descended to earth to play their favourite instruments, just for me. But no phone meant no music this morning, adding to my gloom.

My walking path ran parallel to a hedge with several bends on its way. When I turned on one such bend, a deer stood directly facing me. I am used to seeing plenty of rabbits, pheasants, fowls, and foxes, but deer are uncommon in these fields. Its sudden appearance, at such close quarters, startled me. The last time I'd seen a deer so close was when I visited a zoo. The proximity allowed me to examine the deer's face closely. It looked quizzically at me as if asking me what I was doing on its path.

Soon, two more deer joined in. They were bigger and looked like full-grown adults. We all stood still in total silence, each waiting for the next move from the other. As if the deers could read my mind, they realised their mistake of having trod on alien territory. Suddenly, all three turned around and trotted off into the field.

While I wondered why these deers had veered off their usual path, several more deers jumped out from behind the hedge and followed them into the open fields. I stood there, staring at the herd, the deers looking increasingly smaller as they moved away from me.

Before they became too small to go out of sight, an animal, no bigger than a dog, jumped out of the hedge. I was unsure, at first, what it was. It was also a deer, and from its diminutive size, I guessed it was pretty young. The fawn stood for a moment, looked around and started running in the direction of the herd.

'The fawn has got separated from the rest of the herd, left alone,' I guessed. Soon, it became clear that the fawn was too young to keep up with the herd. The herd kept moving away from the fawn, increasing the gap.

I could not help feeling sad for the poor fawn. While I was secretly hoping it would somehow find the strength to bridge the gap and reunite with its herd, to my dismay, the fawn suddenly stopped. From where I stood, I could not work out what was in the fawn's mind. Suddenly, it started running in a new direction, at an angle from the original, moving further away from the herd.

The fawn had clearly made a wrong decision. I could not understand what made the fawn change direction. Perhaps the fawn had lagged too far behind, and the herd was out of its view. In the process, it probably got disoriented. Or maybe it was distracted by some sound or scent. I got worried about the safety of the fawn. These fields are frequented by dogs; they would find a fawn an easy target to chase and kill for a meal.

I felt an urge to redirect the fawn towards the herd. I burst out shouting, 'Stop!'. *Silly me!* I stood there feeling helpless. The fawn obviously couldn't hear me. My only comfort was that not many dogs were around in the fields at that time.

How I wished the fawn could see the bigger picture as I could!

The fawn kept trotting in the new direction without any sign of slowing down. '*It found an extraordinary burst of energy in its legs, but at the wrong time.*' I could feel the fear in the fawn's heart, running alone in the open fields.

I watched as the fawn disappeared into a ditch next. Would it be the end of the poor fawn? Perhaps it had run out of strength. *Maybe it got injured or broke its legs.* I imagined the fawn lying exhausted at the bottom of the ditch. Soon, it would be a tasty meal for some savage dog.

I breathed a sigh of relief to see the fawn emerging from the ditch. It resumed running into the adjoining field. But it was running further away from its herd. By now, its herd was left far behind. *How long can the baby maintain this sprint, and where will it end?*

I imagined the worst fate for the poor fawn. *No, it could now never unite with his family.* The thought of the exhausted fawn being savagely attacked by dogs sent shivers down my spine. I decided to cut my morning walk short. I knew the face of the poor fawn would haunt me for a long time. I was about to turn around and walk back home.

Then, I spotted another deer that appeared almost miraculously from nowhere, running towards the fawn. The sight of the deer following the fawn raised my hopes. *Ah, finally, the rescue had come for the poor fawn. At least they could get strength from each other's company.*

Given its limited life experience, the fawn on its own must be pretty vulnerable. No doubt, the deer's company would make a difference; it would lift its spirit. Perhaps it would run faster now.

But can the fawn sense the other deer following it? From my higher vantage point, I had a far more expansive view of the field than the fawn. How I wished for the fawn to get somehow a gift of the sight I enjoyed due to my height! If only I could assure the fawn that it would soon have the company of another deer. Desperate, I shouted, 'Don't worry. Company is on the way!'

I was frozen at the site, peering into space. The trees in the distance stood helplessly as mute witnesses to the plight of the fawn and turbulence in my mind. A faint mist, still lingering on the horizon, was slowly melting away as if poised to reveal a secret.

As the image of the hapless, frightened fawn churned inside me, I felt a strange sensation, I had never experienced before, like a phone vibrating in silent mode. Though the feeling was different, out of sheer habit, I thrust my hand into my pocket when I realised, I had no phone with me that day.

I looked up at the sky, wondering: Was it a message for me? And from whom?

While I was searching for the receiver, lying somewhere deep inside, to decode the message someone was sending me from afar, suddenly the penny dropped.

Ah, the vibes of the big picture for me!

Dying Declaration

Dear Mama,

It pains me to no end to know the grief I have caused you from my single mistake. I realise I should have never ventured out on my own that day. The first survival lesson you taught us was to always stick to each other, for the key to our strength is our numbers: we are the eyes and ears for all of us.

That morning, the rabbit had woken up early. He looked around to find he was the only one awake; the others were all still asleep. He remembered the strict instruction from Mama: 'Never go out on your own'. He should have curbed his impatience. He should have waited for others to wake up, and join him in starting the day. *It can't hurt if I just nip out for a peek,* he thought.

He crawled out of the burrow behind the dense thicket and entered a grassy meadow. *What dangers might be lurking there?* He could not see any. With his well-sharpened sight, hearing and smell, the rabbit had blended them into a finely tuned sense of safety versus danger. He was confident he had acquired the most critical tool in his survival kit — an uncanny ability to anticipate danger from a distance. He'd had ample opportunities to practise his survival skills, too. Every time they were put to the test, they had not failed him. Now was his chance to venture into unexplored terrains and frolic to his heart's content. Surely, he would be able to work out an escape route in case danger did strike unexpectedly.

The temptation was too hard to resist. The open heath was so inviting.

The rabbit's self-restraint snapped.

He found himself hopping away. The dark night had just broken into a glorious dawn. The air was crisp and cool. The grass was soft and bouncy. There was no danger in sight. He hopped in abandon without a care in the world. He would go in a straight line for some distance before changing his path and continuing until the next turn of direction. He didn't see anything new, nor did he encounter anything interesting. The heath was unending. No matter which way he wandered, a boundless stretch of green lay in front of him.

A row of houses stood across the heath. Their doors were firmly shut, windows unopened. There was no sign of human activity and no sound of movement. It was too early in the morning. People inside were perhaps busy catching the last lap of their sleep or savouring their dreams. Another edge of the heath backed up to what looked like the gardens of houses across. In one of their gardens, a few ducks swam aimlessly in the pond. The rabbit felt slightly sorry for the ducks, who were still sleeping. They didn't know what they were missing: the blissful interlude between night and day, with its ephemeral blend of soft light and gentle silence. This precious time would soon give way to the blazing brightness and cacophony of the hectic day.

He had never tasted such freedom. The exhilaration of his escapade made him mildly euphoric. He forgot he was a mere rabbit: he felt like a free spirit, uncontainable and invincible. The last thing on his mind was safety.

He found himself at the edge of the green grass, poised to cross the road. He had wandered beyond all the other boundaries of the heath, but he had never crossed this road before. His curiosity over what lay beyond the road prodded him. The next moment, he hopped onto the road.

Suddenly, a gigantic machine moving at lightning speed roared down the road. Its thunderous noise was deafening. It was as big as the houses on the edge of the heath, but unlike the houses, it was on the move.

Everything changed in the blink of an eye.

The rabbit felt a heavy thud. The pain was blinding and wiped out his world. All that was left was darkness, thick and impenetrable.

I lay on the spot for how long, I can't tell. The next experience was too strange to describe. I felt my spirit rising from the road into something soft; it felt like clouds.

'I must be in heaven', I thought. It felt so different from anything I've known. I was floating merrily in the company of an angel for a tour of the new world that would be my home from now on. I forgot my pain altogether. The angel's voice was like a balm, soft and soothing, although I couldn't catch what she was mumbling, let alone understand her. Again, my mental clock failed me. I am not sure how long the tour lasted.

Then something came over me. I sensed a tightening of my chest. My breathing was laboured. In no time, it was inordinately hard to breathe. Next, I couldn't breathe at all. I knew my end had come. But it was confusing. Pain, suffering and distress belonged to the world of mortals. If I were in heaven, how was I still feeling pain?

I must tell you this before it is too late. You made us believe humans were the most diabolical creatures on earth. They are smaller than many animals, but their size is beguiling. They possess tiny explosives that they can fire at will with deadly effect. They are endowed with devious minds which work in mysterious ways. Sometimes, they kill us just for fun. The glow of satisfaction on their face when their explosive hits us defies all explanation. It is hard to understand how the death of one of us gives them so much pleasure. That the sight of the suffering of a dying animal can create ripples of joy in their hearts is mind-boggling.

I accept that your longer life gives you a wealth of experience I can't match. Your wisdom, likewise, is unrivalled. Nevertheless, you have failed to understand humans fully. You have been too quick to judge them. They are not all gun-wielding, blood-thirsty devils incarnate, out to kill us for fun. Mama, humans are two-faced, and it seems you have seen only one. They can be the most caring creatures imaginable, capable of angelic acts.

If I succeed in rectifying your mistaken view of humans, I will have the consolation that my life wasn't wasted. I would depart peacefully in the knowledge that I didn't die in vain.

You must be wondering how I can be so sure. You have to trust me. When we are about to die, we always speak the truth.

Now I know I was muddled about what was going on. The angelic pair of hands that picked me up and comforted me belonged to a human. Eventually, everything fell into place. I know now what happened to me. From the conversation between my saviour and her daughter, I can piece together the short interlude before my death.

A massive lorry hit me while I was crossing the road. The blow to my head was deadly, but it didn't kill me instantly. I was stunned by the impact. When I briefly recovered from the concussion, I tried to run, but I was paralysed and couldn't move. That is when my saviour arrived on the scene. A lady picked me up and carried me in a cushion of her soft linen scarf to her home. For the first time in my life, I was looking at everything from a height. It was surreal, an entirely new viewpoint. It was so different from what I had seen from the ground level. Upon reaching home, she met with her daughter, and they talked briefly. By then, I was gasping for breath. She cannily sensed my end was near. She walked around her garden, holding me close to her bosom until I breathed my last. She stroked me all the time until my body was absolutely still.

I can almost hear you asking: 'How can you be so sure it was a human, not an angel, who comforted you in your dying moments? You were probably too dazed by the knock on your head to know what actually happened.'

Yes, my life was too short to learn everything about angels. Nevertheless, I know something for sure: angels do not weep. No doubt, they are reservoirs of kindness and compassion. But, unlike humans, their hearts are made of unique stuff: they never melt into tears.

But she was weeping. I felt her tears drop on my back. I thought it was raining then, but I realised my mistake when I was put to rest in her garden. The garden was dry.

These were the last thoughts of the dying rabbit.

There lay his body, silenced forever, resting in the lap of the loving care lavished on him until the very last flicker of his life was snuffed out.

Absolute Intelligence : The New AI

My laptop pinged.

Do you want me to tell you a story?

Every time I turn on my laptop, a message appears on the screen. It usually reads something like, 'What is on your mind today?' or 'What is the joke of the day?' I generally ignore such inane messages and move on.

Do you want me to tell you a story?

The message today was slightly different; it had a personal touch. I might have been tempted to oblige on another day, but it was definitely not the day for stories. My head was bursting with more serious stuff, saturated with facts and figures, leaving me in no mood to indulge in fiction.

As a scientist, research grants are my lifeblood. My professional progress hinges on a string of successful grant applications that secure salaries for my team, including my own. Even before a new project gets underway, my mind will already be working on the subsequent study. The success of the following grant application ensures the continuity of my studies, as it guarantees the next tranche of funding. Fortunately, I have never had a long fallow period. My prolonged spree of grant applications has yielded a seamless succession of funded studies without interruption for years. My research career has not merely survived the cut and thrust of the brutal funding process; it has flourished in its frantic rush. Well, until now, as my luck seemed to have run out. I have been stumped by my current grant application.

For months, I have been grappling with the application for a grand project on which I am the principal investigator. My area of expertise is mathematics, and my field of study is quantum computing. I had successfully teamed up with researchers from two other disciplines, psychology and genetics. I had planned an ambitious project with a grand scope and a multi-stage study spanning about ten years. However, as its scope expanded, the progress of the project slowed.

The atmosphere in the bigger team started collegially, and disagreements were ironed out quickly. As the team expanded and other disciplines joined, the group became less cohesive. Differences turned into disputes, and varying perspectives developed into discords. Soon, cracks in consensus started appearing on key steps of the project. Call it turf wars or a fight for supremacy; settling arguments has become progressively more challenging. Over time, I've ended up devoting less time to scholarship and more to conflict resolution. The atmosphere has turned increasingly acrimonious, and the study has stalled.

The project has undergone several revisions, and the latest grant application has gone through a series of drafts. But the end is still nowhere in sight. It has been a race against time to meet the application deadline, and my patience is wearing thin. By its extent in scope, duration and, most importantly, funding, completing this mammoth study is a crucial step in my progress up the academic ladder. It is no exaggeration to say that my professional life hinges on its success.

Crunch time has arrived to finalise the application. Reluctantly, I have concluded that our collaborative team project must be disbanded. I called an emergency meeting and made a snap announcement that the grand project was off. In its place, I have decided to go solo with a modified version of the project. But this is easier said than done. Now, I have the daunting task of rewriting the application in a matter of days.

As I contemplate redrafting it as a slim-lined study, it no longer sounds exciting. It is no longer ground-breaking in scope nor novel in design. I would probably reject it for funding if I were a judge on the approval panel. *Have I killed off the project*?

Anyway, as I closed the window on the computer screen, the message about the story pinged again. The process repeated itself, and by the third or the fourth round, instead of closing the window, I responded 'No'.

I thought that was the end of it.

Annoyingly, the message refused to go away. I again stared at the question on the screen:

Do you want me to tell you a story?

I was dying to start on a fresh grant application. But I felt trapped. I had no choice but to listen to this story. The machine's persistence was exasperating. How dare this goddamn contraption impose some stupid story on me! Do I lack the brains to know what I need? Can't I have the last word?

This affront to my autonomy enraged me. How can this story be more important than my research grant application? I was determined to defy the machine's insistence on the story.

I was ready to fight and replied in all caps: 'NO'.

The following message on the screen set my blood to boil.

Do you want me to tell you a story?

This drove me insane. On an impulse, I picked up the laptop, and with all my might, smashed it on the ground. It split open, its components broken into pieces. The screen fragmented into smithereens strewn across the floor.

I sat on my chair, staring at the catastrophic result of my rage, horrified at the enormity of my mistake. But what happened next was nothing short of miraculous. I didn't know what to make of it.

As if drawn by an invisible, magical force, the laptop's splintered parts pulled themselves together and reassembled back to their original structure.

I was least prepared for such high drama. Nonetheless, seeing my precious laptop intact again gave me instant relief. However, I was spooked by the laptop's behaviour, as if it had acquired a spark of life. The unearthly scene gave me a jolt, pushing me back on my chair. It felt like I was watching a video clip of an exploding laptop played backwards.

Is it real?

I shook my head to make sure of what I was seeing.

Next, as if it was simply reversing its trajectory, the laptop flew up and sat back on my desk.

The reassembly of the laptop was a miracle, and I assumed that was enough for the day. I did not know what to expect next. Would it still function? I looked at the screen.

The same question that had provoked my fury and the cataclysmic act of destruction reappeared on the screen.

Now, I knew what to answer, but I was paralysed with fear.

As if it could sense my fright, the message on the screen changed to soothe my nerves.

This story is highly recommended for you.

This placatory message appeared to have the desired effect; I felt my composure slowly returning. But I was intrigued by the machine's assertion and wondered: Where does it get its authority from? *How does it know what is good for me?*

I managed to collect myself enough to respond, 'Yes'.

Somewhat dazed, I remained glued to the computer screen as if my gaze would tie it to the tabletop and stop it from flying back to the floor.

The story started with a rather drab beginning.

There was once a professor working at a prestigious university. He was highly regarded in his field and a world authority in his study area. In scholarly circles, he was held in awe for his academic prowess and acerbic wit. But only those in his inner circle knew of his serious character flaw: his very foul temper. He didn't suffer fools gladly and didn't mince his words if he was crossed or questioned without sufficient grounds.

At home, his temper was at its most vile. He had a broken marriage and lived with his long-suffering servant, who, unfortunately, was at the receiving end of the professor's short fuse. The slightest mistake by the servant would set him off; he would shout at him. His abusive behaviour didn't stop there. If he did not get his way, he would not hesitate to resort to physical violence. The poor servant tried hard not to upset the professor and stuck to him, perhaps out of loyalty.

One day, the professor returned from work early. But he expected his dinner to be ready when he reached home.

'Why is the dinner not ready?' the professor screamed.

'Forgive me, Sir. I was busy today tidying up the house. I shall put the meat in the oven; it will be ready in forty minutes.'

'Forty minutes wait!' the professor fumed.

He was incandescent with rage and struck the servant with a mighty blow. It was so violent that the servant collapsed instantly. The servant was, in fact, dead from the massive blow. The professor was little bothered by the macabre incident. He made no attempt to revive the servant. He calmly proceeded to bury him in a shallow grave in the garden and returned to his house. The professor went on with his evening routine, totally unperturbed.

The next day, he went to work as if nothing untoward had happened. When he returned home, a rather gory sight greeted him. His servant dug himself out of the grave in the garden and walked into the house. He received the professor in his customary way and announced, 'Dinner is ready'. As the professor sat at the dining table, the servant pulled the dish out of the oven and put it in front of him. The professor ate it without a word.

The story's eerie plot gripped me as I visualised the dead servant rising out of the grave and trundling along the garden towards the oven. I could almost see him taking the dish out and serving it to the professor.

The professor's household routine rolled on as if everything was normal. But the meat from the oven served to the professor, day after day, started to shrivel.

It dried into a dark leather-like stuff. It must be tasting horrible, too.

'But the professor did not have to eat it. Couldn't he say no?' I piped in.

No, he had no choice but to eat it.

The meat soon got putrefied, and it smelt rotten. But the professor had to put it into his mouth silently without protest.

Several days passed, and this routine was repeated until hardly any meat was left on the dish. It had decomposed into a miasma of organic matter swarming in maggots with a horrible stench. For a dish of food, it was the most revolting sight imaginable.

'Surely, the professor could not eat what was no longer edible.'

'No, he had to eat what was put on the table. After all, that was the dinner he had demanded. Although the mild-mannered servant looked meek, under the circumstances, his unspoken instructions were too imposing to ignore.'

'So, how long could he carry on eating the decomposed food?' I could not resist asking.

'Till he dropped dead.'

The computer screen went blank. And so did my mind. The chilling story had frozen my thought process. I thought I was watching a horror movie.

I couldn't take my eyes off the gadget on my desk. I intently watched for the next flicker of activity, or should I say, a sign of new life. My laptop seemed to have metamorphosed into an enigmatic creature with paranormal powers. Underneath its inert exterior, I imagined an intricate array of frantic actions in its inner organs, working furiously towards launching its next episode of horror. Amidst the day's freakish backdrop, I did not know what might spring from this new specimen. I sat petrified on my chair, dreading the next wave of terror in this gruesome spectacle.

I had goosebumps, wondering if the next ping would read: Do you want to hear another story?

But nothing of the sort happened.

Whatever intelligence lurked behind the featureless screen seemed content that a single story was enough to drive the message home.

Is this the height of AI?

The laptop pinged again.

No, this is not the AI as we know it. It is

Absolute intelligence.

Author's Note: The sub-story of the professor within the story's plot is taken from a BBC radio play I heard while driving to work some years ago. It made such an impression that I have taken the liberty of using it as a parable within my story, although it is not my creation. As I missed both the play's beginning and end, I have no clue as to the play's title or writer. Hence, this is my only acknowledgement of the unknown author.

Dog's Story

We have heard phrases like dog's dinner and dog's life, although we are somewhat uncertain of their exact meaning today. But the dog's story is plainly absurd because dogs can't talk. However, this doesn't apply to the world where not only can dogs speak, but stones can sing, and trees can think. Here, the living and non-living are not so distinct: all things including lakes, mountains and clouds, are conscious. That is where this story comes from.

Why am I telling you my story? Not least, this will confirm what you have always felt somewhere deep down that dog is man's best friend. But do you know the lengths a dog would go to for its master? A first-person account of a dog's capability and loyalty may surprise you.

Like most stories, this one has multiple versions. While the event in question remains the same, we all see it differently. Sometimes, it takes an inordinate amount of effort to get to the truth, and it still falls short for some.

***

The most widely known version of this story appeared in the local newspaper.

Tragic Deaths of Dog Lover George Walker
and His Dog, Smoky, in a Freak Accident

Last Sunday evening, 57-year-old George Walker, a

frequent sight in the local mountains, in the company of his large Golden Retriever, Smoky, accidentally plunged from a height. Whilst walking, George slipped and fell down a cliff. His dog, Smoky, securely tied in a harness, got dragged with George.

A rock-climbing exercise was underway around the cliff, with the climbing gear in position. They were seen dangling from the ropes, high up in the air, for several minutes. Somewhat miraculously, they became entangled in the ropes and slings attached to a peg in the rocks, and they were seen dangling from the ropes, high up in the air, for several minutes. But all hopes of their survival were dashed. The peg on the rock was not secure enough to bear the weight of George and Smoky. While attempts to save them were underway, the peg loosened and came off before they could be rescued. Sadly, in the end, both plunged to their deaths.

But this is nowhere near the full story.

***

For Daniel McSwain, the climbing group leader on the scene who witnessed the accident, it was devastating. He was confident, till the end, that at least George could be saved. With Daniel's expertise in rock climbing and some quick thinking, he thought he could come to George's aid and give him the gift of life. His extensive experience gave him a keen sense of the maximum weight the peg could bear. George was a slight man, thin as a wire, whereas the dog was a massive Golden Retriever, almost as heavy as George. Daniel was doubtful if the peg could bear the combined weight of George and the dog. But, he was confident it could support one of them long enough to allow a rescue team time to reach them. And, if a choice had to be made between man and dog, the answer was obvious.

However, Daniel was puzzled about what really transpired in those crucial few minutes. He had a clear line of communication with George. His instructions to George were unequivocal: cut the dog off the rope because that was the only way to save his own life. He was confident George received his instructions and understood exactly what needed to be done. No doubt, the situation was dire, but from their conversation over the phone, George sounded composed in his responses. Even from such a height, the knife in his hand was visible; you could see its sharp blade shining in the glare of the afternoon sun. George had both the opportunity and the time to cut the dog off, but that did not happen. Although he appeared to remain calm, perhaps he lost his nerve. Or did he freeze out of panic?

Daniel later learned that George had suffered an extensive injury to his internal organs. But the injury to his right arm stood out. While his forearm was relatively unscathed, his hand had been mutilated; it looked like he had suffered a frenzied animal bite. The most likely culprit was the dog, whose bite must have stopped George from cutting the rope in time. 'Poor animal!' Daniel thought. 'The dumb dog didn't have a clue as to what was going on.'

'*But how can you blame the dog?* Daniel reflected; the wretched thing could not foresee the consequences of its actions. All it could do was to act reflexively'. *That is how humans set themselves apart from animals.* The superior human mind can set goals and plan a sequence of actions to achieve them. Human brains have evolved to suppress their animal instincts at critical junctures and work on a thought-out plan logically.

At the bottom of the cliff, a monument was commissioned at the accident site to commemorate the bond between George and Smoky, known locally as the inseparable pair. In its centre, on a pedestal, stood a life-size bronze figure of the slightly built George next to the massive Smoky. Whenever Daniel passed by it, his gaze was drawn to the pair. He could not help noticing the mismatch in their size, but their body language showed they were in perfect harmony.

***

Here is the inside story from Smoky's mouth.

When I woke up from my sleep, I found myself in a cloud of mist. Through the haze, I spotted a man at a distance in conversation with a group; they listened to him in rapt attention. He didn't speak much, as if he knew precisely how much was enough. They dispersed one by one. After the last person left, he turned towards me. Soon, I could see him clearly. He had a distinguished look and a dignified presence. I was instantly drawn to him.

'Where am I?' I asked him.

'You can call it The Land of Angels.'

'And you are?'

'Take me as the local guide here to orient you to this new world. I will be meeting George next after we finish.'

'You seem to be more than a guide. Shall I call you The Chief?'

'You may if it makes you happy.'

My head felt fuzzy, and I could not remember how I got there. He comforted me, saying, 'It is natural to lose your bearings when you leave your familiar world for a new one.' His gentle demeanour put me at ease and helped me piece together fragments of my memory of what happened to me. As my patchy memory coalesced, a clearer picture of the events emerged.

I died in an accident while out walking with George. I remember walking one minute and hanging at the end of a rope high up in the air the next. I saw George by my side, hanging at the end of another rope. He spoke with Daniel, the leader of the rock climbing group, about help coming our way. His tone was frantic, but it was a relief to hear that Daniel was arranging a rescue operation.

What happened next was terrifying. George continued speaking with Daniel and took out a knife. Soon after, he started cutting his rope. Daniel's voice was steady and full of authority. Calmly, he told George that the peg supporting our ropes was loose and could give way at any time unless the load was made lighter. It could support the weight of George alone. Daniel's instruction to George was unequivocal: he must cut my rope so that he would survive. Otherwise, the peg would give way to our combined weight, killing both of us.

I knew George could not imagine his life without me. I could read his mind. He surmised that if only one of us would survive, it must be me. So, for George, the solution was simple, and the decision was easy: he had to cut his own rope off.

I saw the steely determination in George's eyes. He was intent on executing his final plan of action: to cut himself off so my life would be spared. For me, the unfolding disaster was too painful to contemplate. George would fall to his death, and that would save my life. But what life would I have when he was gone? I scratched my brain in a panic. What could I do, high up in the air, hanging by a rope? I did the only thing in my power. I bit his hand hard to make him drop the knife.

The Chief was curious about why I was at pains to tell my story.

'I want the world to know you can't separate the dog from the man for long. We would do anything, even maul our master, if that were what it would take to keep us together. And dog remains man's best friend, even in the world of angels, where no statue is needed to celebrate their inseparability. We are living proof, even if we have to die to demonstrate it. Now humans can confidently vouch for its universality.'

'Anything else?' asked the Chief.

'That is not all. We can also read our master's thoughts – like best friends do.'

Now, you have got this straight from the dog's mouth.

'But you hesitated in biting him. What was holding you back?'

'It was not easy. It was actually the hardest decision of my life. You know how difficult it is to bite the hand that feeds you?'

'Well, it was a relief to see that you succeeded in the end.'

'Yes, but it was tough. George started fighting me when he realised what I was going to do.'

'I was moved,' the Chief said, 'to see how set you both were on saving the other's life at your own expense.'

'That is what best friends do, don't they?'

While I was in conversation with the Chief, his assistant came in with some fresh news. It was George's final post-mortem report. He had sustained extensive head and multiple organ injuries. Further analysis confirmed he had been suffering from terminal cancer.

'So, if the accident had not happened, the cancer would have killed him in a matter of months,' the assistant commented.

I looked at the Chief, and a faint smile flickered across his face. It was the kind you give when you are told something you already know.

'You were right. George did not have much life left. The alternative to the accident was a painful and protracted death.'

'So, you already knew he was dying of cancer?'

The Chief gave another of his knowing smiles with a slight nod.

I realised how wretched my life would have been if the accident had not happened. Without George, My life would have been desolate.

The Chief looked away briefly as if he was distracted by something pressing that just came to his mind. Or maybe he was simply avoiding eye contact.

'So, the accident, however tragic it might appear, was indeed a blessing,' I said.

'Yes, I have no doubt, without George, your life would have been an absolute misery. I reckoned this was the most humane treatment for you two,' the Chief said.

I was about to say, 'Dangling high up in the air, I was praying to God to grant some strength to my bite,' when I suddenly realised where I had landed.

I wanted to thank the Chief and say, 'I can see now who gave me the strength to bite George's hand.'

But, in a flash, the blanket of haze was back, the Chief lost in its midst.

Black Eagle Books

www.blackeaglebooks.org
info@blackeaglebooks.org

Black Eagle Books, an independent publisher, was founded as
a nonprofit organization in April, 2019. It is our mission to
connect and engage the Indian diaspora and the world at
large with the best of works of world literature published on
a collaborative platform, with special emphasis on
foregrounding Contemporary Classics and New Writing.